Jill Bartlett, nurse on board the Greek cruise ship the *Hellene*, is well aware of the dangers of shipboard romances. But is her relationship with Dr David Harcourt really nothing more than a light-hearted flirtation inspired by the magic of the Mediterranean?

CRUISE NURSE

BY
CLARE LAVENHAM

MILLS & BOON LIMITED
London · Sydney · Toronto

First published in Great Britain 1983
by Mills & Boon Limited, 15–16 Brook's Mews,
London W1A 1DR

ISBN 0 263 74290 3

Set in 11 on 12½ pt Linotron Times
03/0583

Photoset by Rowland Phototypesetting Ltd
Bury St Edmunds, Suffolk
Made and printed in Great Britain by
Richard Clay (The Chaucer Press) Ltd
Bungay, Suffolk

CHAPTER ONE

IT WAS all so beautiful, so like a dream come true, that Jill could scarcely believe it was real. She stood leaning against the rail on the top deck, the early morning breeze gently ruffling her short copper-coloured hair, and stared with enchanted eyes at the loveliness all around.

Blue sea—the incredible dark blue of the Mediterranean—and overhead a wide expanse of blue sky without a cloud to be seen. A big white ship, steady as a rock beneath her feet, and no other living person in sight. It was all hers, to wonder at and enjoy.

Jill had arrived late the previous evening, flying from London and joining the ship at Genoa. Her plane had been delayed and she had gone to bed after a very late dinner and a quick look round. It had been dark and the April night distinctly chilly. Tired and a little homesick, she had thought nostalgically of the interesting jobs her agency work had brought her. Wasn't it just possible she might find her new job as ship's nurse both frustrating and boring after the drama of acute illness?

But this morning her mood had changed completely, and even her apparent solitude didn't make her feel lonely.

A sudden loud splash told her that she wasn't alone after all. There was a swimming pool further forward and someone had just dived in. Curiously, Jill looked to see who else was up so early but she could only make out a pair of flailing arms as the swimmer did a rapid crawl round and round the small space available. Sunshine gleamed on a wet dark head, it looked like a man but she couldn't be sure.

Later on, when he had climbed out and was towelling himself vigorously, she discovered that it *was* a man. Tall, broad-shouldered, with a magnificent tan and clad in brief bathing trunks, he looked like an advertisement for a holiday cruise as he stood outlined against sea and sky.

Jill smiled at her flight of fancy and turned to go below. At the top of the steps leading to the next deck down she hesitated.

She had discovered last night that members of the crew ran down these ladder-like steps as though they had been ordinary stairs, whereas passengers climbed laboriously down them backwards. It seemed a good moment to try and emulate the agility of the sailors and Jill put a cautious foot on the first step. Feeling very insecure with nothing to hold on to, she began a careful descent and found herself moving downwards faster and faster. Disaster came three steps from the bottom. Her foot slipped, she took a desperate leap into space and landed awkwardly on hands and knees with one foot twisted under her.

As she struggled to her feet, furious at her own idiocy, there was a sharp pain in her ankle and she was obliged to cling to the nearest rail.

To her mortification, the lower deck was not entirely unoccupied and a young man in jeans and a red tee-shirt came hurrying towards her.

'Mees is hurt?' The voice was definitely foreign and very dark eyes gazed at her solicitously.

'A little. I seem to have twisted my ankle.' Jill looked down ruefully and found it was already swelling.

'Is not broken?' He knelt before her and began to unfasten her sandal. 'Better to take this off, I think.'

He had black hair, very thick and curly, and she guessed he was probably Greek, since the *Hellene* belonged to a Greek line. Noting that he was physically attractive but not at that moment in the least interested, Jill sat down on the steps and started a gentle massage.

It really was an absolutely maddening thing to happen on her first morning, and all her own fault too.

'I'm sure it's only sprained, thank goodness. Hopefully, it'll probably be all right soon.' She glanced up into the liquid brown eyes and forced a smile.

Above her head another voice spoke suddenly.

'Excuse me—' The swimmer, now wearing an orange towelling jacket, was coming down the steps swiftly, displaying all the expertise which Jill had so sadly lacked.

She moved to one side and he passed her at a run, reached the deck and then stopped.

'What's the matter? Have you hurt yourself?'

'Just slightly. I slipped on the steps,' she told him curtly.

'I'm not surprised.' The new arrival looked Jill up and down scornfully. 'I saw you start off and I thought you'd probably come to grief. You'd better let me have a look at that ankle.'

Intensely annoyed at his tone, she put her chin haughtily in the air. 'I've already decided it's only sprained, thank you.'

'I don't suppose you're a very good judge.' As the other man had done, he knelt down and put his fingers in a masterful way, and yet very gently, on the swollen ankle.

Some of Jill's fury with herself seemed to be augmenting her instinctive dislike of this high-handed stranger.

'Leave me alone!' She struggled to her feet. 'I'll go down to my cabin and put a bandage on. I'm sure it will be perfectly all right in no time.'

He raised his head and stared at her. For a moment his dark grey eyes, black-lashed and as cold as the North Sea in winter, held her gaze with a magnetism she couldn't help being aware of, and then he rose to his feet in one lithe movement.

'Okay—if you want to be a silly little fool, I'm certainly not going to try and stop you.'

She watched him stride away across the deck, reach another flight of steps and disappear. Turning to the silent onlooker, she was surprised to find him struggling with amusement.

'What's so funny?' she asked coldly.

'If Mees but knew!'

'How can I know if you don't tell me?' She took a step towards him and winced as her ankle objected strongly. 'Please explain why you're laughing. I know I've been a fool but I don't find it in the least amusing.'

He came nearer and slipped his arm in hers. 'Is better this way. I will tell you the joke as we go along.'

'Thank you.' She was glad of his support and at the same time found his nearness a little disturbing. 'Do let me into the secret now,' she begged as he continued to smile broadly.

'First I will introduce myself. I am Toni, the photographer on the *Hellene*. All day I photograph fat people who are not young, and then I go down to the dark room and work there.' He sighed. 'Is a very hard life.'

'I'm sure they're not all fat,' Jill protested.

'Many, many passengers are. Is my lucky day when I find a beautiful girl.' And he added very softly, 'Like you.'

It was impossible not to be pleased at the compliment though Jill was well aware that her looks were nothing out of the ordinary. Her face was too round and her nose too short. Her hair was a beautiful glowing colour but she should have had green eyes to go with it instead of hazel. Maybe her figure wasn't so bad but she had always longed to be taller.

'You will please to tell me your name,' Toni was saying.

'Jill Bartlett. I'm working on the ship too, or at least I shall be later on this morning. I'm the new nurse.'

To her astonishment he halted and stared at her, and then began to laugh more than ever.

'You the new nurse? But this is much funnier than I had understood.'

'I'm glad you're enjoying it,' she snapped, her patience at an end.

Toni was instantly sober. 'Do not be angry with me, Jill. I will explain!' He paused to find the right words. 'The man who wished to examine your ankle—he is the ship's doctor. He is called David Harcourt and he is your new boss. I

think he will not at all like that you treated him
so—so unkindly.'

Jill looked at him in horror. 'Oh dear—how
awful! Why on earth didn't you tell me at the
time?'

'I did not know who *you* were then.'

Jill said no more but her thoughts were turbu-
lent as dismay engulfed her. More than ever she
regretted that absurd attempt to display a non-
existent skill. It was a terribly bad beginning to
her new life and no doubt Dr Harcourt's scorn
would be doubled when he discovered that his
new nurse was such a fool.

By painful degrees they reached the promenade deck, where a few determined-looking
passengers were already walking round and
round, clocking up a mile before breakfast.
From there she could take a lift to her cabin on
'C' deck, Jill recollected thankfully.

'I don't think I need bother you any more.' She
halted as they left the bright sunshine and entered an area red-carpeted just like in a hotel.
'You've been very kind.'

'Is my pleasure to assist pretty girls.' Toni
sketched a bow. 'Why you not want me to take
you to your cabin?'

'Because it's not necessary,' Jill told him
firmly. 'Please go back to the top deck and enjoy
your leisure while you can. I shall be all right.'

As he hesitated the lift stopped beside them

and the doors slid back to reveal a slender girl clad in a black leotard. She had a small pointed face and a mass of golden curls.

'Hi, Danielle!' The photographer greeted her cheerfully. 'This is Jill and she has hurt her ankle. It would be kind to see her safely to her cabin.' He grinned cheekily, showing very white teeth. 'She does not wish that I accompany her.'

He had made her appear ridiculously prudish, Jill thought crossly, and was relieved when Danielle immediately retorted that she could quite understand *that*.

'What happened?' she asked as the lift doors closed behind them.

Jill told her briefly, making no mention of the doctor and not disguising her disgust with herself.

'I do hope it won't ruin your holiday for you,' Danielle said.

'I'm not on holiday.' Once more she explained about her new job. 'What about you?'

'I'm a dancer—Danielle Lestrange. It's not my real name but I always use it. At this moment I'm supposed to be jogging round the promenade deck and I'm very grateful to you for cutting my exercise time short. The other three dancers never have to bother with it but I have this tiresome tendency to put on weight.' She glanced down at herself disparagingly.

'You look slim enough to me.'

'That's because I'm for ever watching the scales. Which is your cabin?'

Jill gave her the number and they moved slowly towards it. As she searched for the key in her handbag, Danielle told her that the dancers were all accommodated one deck further down.

'Inside cabins, of course, just like yours. Considering how hard we work, I think they might treat us rather better, don't you?'

'It's the only thing that has disappointed me so far—not having a view of the sea.' Jill limped into the prettily-furnished little cabin and subsided thankfully into the armchair. 'But the air-conditioning is very good so I can't really complain. It's lovely having my own shower.'

'You're lucky—we have to share.' Danielle looked into the toilet annexe. 'What are you going to do for your ankle? Put a cold compress on it?'

'I haven't got anything suitable.'

'For crying out loud! What's stopping you going along to the surgery and getting something? I expect you've got your own key.'

'Not yet, and I don't want to bother the doctor,' Jill said hastily. 'I've got a few first-aid things I usually take around with me and among them there's a crêpe bandage. It will do very well.'

'I won't offer to put it on for you because I wouldn't be any good at it.' Danielle sat down on the narrow bed and watched as Jill hunted in a drawer. 'It's really rather funny that you should be your own first patient, isn't it? I should think David Harcourt will be amused too.'

Jill said nothing. She was concentrating very hard on applying the bandage with professional skill.

'What's he like?' she asked at last.

'The doctor? Haven't you met him then?'

'Er—not officially. I mean, I've seen him but—'

To her relief Danielle did not allow her to finish the sentence.

'Then you'll have noticed he's a marvellous-looking guy. But I suppose what you really want to know is what he'll be like to work with and I can't tell you that. I don't know anything about him professionally.'

Was there a slight suggestion of evasion in her tone? Jill glanced up and was surprised to find Danielle looking at her with troubled eyes.

'I've worked on several different ships, Jill, and it's my experience that there's generally something odd about the doctor. A truly dedicated type doesn't take that sort of job. Treating tummy upsets and minor injuries must be terribly boring and to my mind a doctor who really wanted to *work* would choose a shore job.'

'It's a good way of travelling and getting paid

for it,' Jill argued. 'There's nothing wrong in that.'

'No, of course not, and sometimes you come across a young doctor straight from hospital who says quite frankly that he wants to travel. But the older ones—even those only slightly older, like David Harcourt—usually have a different reason for going to sea.'

'Like what?'

'Well, it's a sort of escapism. Something's happened to them that they don't like and they want to get away and forget it. Or it could be a woman—'

Jill looked up with a disbelieving smile. 'I reckon you're just theorising. Unless ships' doctors make a habit of pouring out their troubles to you, you can't possibly know anything about it.'

'I'm interested in people and I like trying to find out what makes them tick.'

'And have you discovered what makes Dr Harcourt tick?'

Danielle shook her curls. 'He's a man of mystery as far as his past is concerned. One thing's for sure though—'

'What?' Jill asked curiously as the dancer hesitated.

'He's not nearly as uninterested in the female sex as the passengers probably imagine, so if he makes a pass at you, love, don't say you haven't been warned.'

As Jill stared at her in blank amazement, she jumped up and flexed her muscles. 'Thanks to you, it's much too late for me to go jogging now. I'll pop along to my cabin for a moment and then help you get to the dining room for breakfast. We're supposed to have our meals earlier than the passengers.'

She was back very quickly, wearing a Greek embroidered tunic over her leotard. The lift took them up to the deck on which the vast and glittering dining room was situated.

It was a brilliant scene, more suitable as a setting for a banquet than breakfast. The electric chandeliers all blazed, since there was no daylight, and the tablecloths were of dazzling whiteness. On every table silver vases filled with red and pink carnations added to the general effect of festivity.

'Our tables are over there, near the kitchens,' Danielle said, leading the way.

Hobbling after her, Jill saw a tall man coming towards them, having apparently just finished his breakfast. A look of surprise crossed his face when he recognised the limping girl and he paused in front of her.

'You ought to be resting that ankle,' he said brusquely.

She put her chin in the air and faced him defiantly. 'You can't blame me for wanting some food.'

'You could have had breakfast in your cabin.'

It had never occurred to her and she wouldn't have wanted to shut herself up there anyway. 'I didn't think it was necessary,' she told him loftily.

He was staring down at the injured foot and not paying much attention to what she was saying.

'You seem to have made a good job of that bandage,' he commented with what sounded like very reluctant approval. 'But if the swelling hasn't started to go down by tomorrow you'd better come along to the surgery and get some professional attention. It's open from nine-thirty to eleven.'

'Yes, I know.'

She simply *must* tell him now! Jill took a deep breath and prepared to make her confession, but it was too late. David was already striding towards the exit and, with a shrug, she limped on her way.

Danielle had joined three girls at a round table and she waved to Jill.

'Come and join us and I'll introduce you.'

They were all dancers and, in different ways, as attractive as Danielle. Martine had ash-blonde hair, Helen was a redhead and Jeanette's hair was a glossy black. They accepted Jill's presence without much interest and continued to talk among themselves, making frank and mostly unflattering comments on the passengers.

'They look a dull lot—mostly geriatrics,' Martine said scornfully.

'The older ones are usually better at enjoying themselves than the others,' Danielle argued. 'I think the worst age group is the thirties and forties who have got it made. They expect an awful lot.'

'They've got the most lolly though,' Jeanette pointed out. 'And they don't mind throwing it around.'

Helen tossed back her long red hair. 'To my mind the worst of all are the young couples who're only interested in each other. I like attractive young blokes to take an interest in *me*.'

Jill listened and made no attempt to join in. It seemed probable that the dancers would get a lot more social life than was likely to come the nurse's way, but she wouldn't let that bother her. She wasn't looking for romance; in fact, she intended to do her best to avoid it. Most of her friends had warned her—some laughingly, some in earnest—against shipboard flirtations.

The dancers left the table before she had finished, apparently to spend the morning rehearsing in the big deserted lounge. Not sorry to be alone, she lingered over her coffee until her watch informed her it was time to get ready for work.

It was a painful journey back to her cabin and the passengers going into breakfast all looked at her curiously. Her dark blue uniform dress was hanging in the cupboard and she changed quickly, rolling up the sleeves and donning a pair of starched white cuffs. The shipping company hadn't seemed to mind what she wore so long as it was a recognisable nursing outfit.

Fortunately the medical department was on the same deck, only a short distance away. The door stood open and, as she paused, she found herself looking into a small waiting room. On the left another door was also open and she saw a conventional consulting room, with desk, examination couch and screen. It, too, was empty.

David Harcourt must be here somewhere. Jill limped as far as the doorway of the second room. As she wondered whether to announce her presence by calling out, he appeared from yet another room beyond. He was wearing an immaculate white coat with his stethoscope hanging from his neck, and greeted her at once in quite a friendly tone.

'I was hoping you'd get here in good time, Nurse, so I could show you round—' His voice died away and he stared at Jill in dismay. 'Good God—it's you!'

'I'm afraid so,' Jill said apologetically.

CHAPTER TWO

'WHY on earth didn't you tell me?' David exploded.

Jill conjured up a nervous smile. 'There doesn't seem to have been an opportunity.'

He raised his eyebrows at that, thick level brows which came near to meeting in the middle. 'That's a matter of opinion. And I don't know what you're doing here anyway. I told you to rest.'

'I can surely survive one and a half hours of surgery, especially as we may not get any patients.' Her apologetic manner had immediately changed to unconcealed mutiny. 'After that I'll find a deck chair and stretch out in the sun, I promise you.'

'I hope you're not always as obstinate as this,' he said drily. 'I expect my nurses to carry out my orders, not do their own prescribing.'

'So I would if I didn't happen to be the patient.' Jill took a step forward, trying not to wince. 'May I look round now, please? I've never seen a medical department on a ship before.'

'The *Hellene* has a very good one.' He immediately became very professional. 'This door leads to a small ward, with room for three patients, and there's also an operating theatre for real emergencies.'

'Have you ever had any?' she asked as she looked admiringly at the miniature ward with its three beds neatly made up, the lockers and bed tables in position, exactly like those in a shore hospital.

'We had an appendicectomy on the last trip, a very straightforward job. Fortunately the nurse who was here temporarily was extremely competent and she was able to act as anaesthetist.'

Perhaps Jill was unduly sensitive but his tone had suggested to her that he had serious doubts in his mind about her own competence.

'What happened to her? I mean, why was she only temporary?'

'Because that was what she wanted. She came here at very short notice to fill a gap which occurred when the previous nurse—er—had to go home suddenly for urgent personal reasons.'

'I see,' Jill said thoughtfully, not because she actually saw anything—though she sensed a mystery—but because some comment was required of her.

David gave her a sharp look and then went back to the surgery and unlocked a drawer in the desk.

'Here are your keys, one for the outer door

and the other for the drugs cupboard. You may use that on your own authority if I should happen to be ashore and somebody needs attention. But you must not, of course, issue anything except the ordinary pain-killers, laxatives and so on.'

'I was wondering about going ashore. I know the ship calls at quite a lot of places. Shall I be able to do any sight-seeing?'

'Not at present,' he told her firmly.

Jill flushed. 'I know perfectly well that I couldn't manage it just now, but my ankle will soon be okay again. I've never been to Greece before and I hope very much I shall be able to see something of it.'

'Oh yes, of course you will,' David assured her. 'I'm not a slave-driver. You'll be free to go ashore at all the ports of call for a couple of hours or so, probably longer if you wish. But you'll have to miss out Corfu—our first port—this time because of your sprain.'

He was staring at her in a commanding sort of way and Jill dropped her eyes meekly. They wouldn't reach Corfu until the day after tomorrow and her ankle might be better by then, but she thought it inadvisable to mention the possibility just at the moment. Instead she asked whether it was considered necessary for one or the other of them always to be in attendance in case any passenger needed medical help.

'In theory—yes, but in actual fact the Staff

Captain is very reasonable about it. In the event of our both wanting to go ashore at the same time, there would be no objection provided most of the passengers were ashore too. Several members of the crew are trained in first-aid and could cope with anything which arose during our absence.'

It all sounded just about perfect, Jill reflected. The one snag was the intense dislike they felt for each other. Dr Harcourt obviously considered her an incompetent fool, and she had definitely decided that he was stiff-necked, bossy and intolerant. Not at all the sort of epithets which should be applicable to a doctor.

As they waited for patients she balanced her weight on one leg—ignoring his frown of disapproval—and busied herself with becoming thoroughly acquainted with the contents of the various drawers and cupboards so that, if something was required in a hurry, she would be able to find it without delay.

Half an hour later a sudden long blast on the ship's siren startled her into an exclamation of astonishment.

'What on earth's that?'

David raised his head from the medical journal he was studying. 'Don't you really know?'

'I wouldn't have asked if I did.'

'There's always a boat drill the first morning at sea,' he said impatiently. 'It's announced in

English, German and French and I can't imagine why you seem to have heard nothing. I suppose you've located your life-jacket in the bottom of the cupboard in your cabin, read the instructions and know which is your boat station?'

To her annoyance Jill felt herself turning slowly pink. This hateful man was constantly putting her at a disadvantage.

'I saw it there last night,' she told him curtly, 'but this morning I've been much too busy spraining my ankle to think any more about it. I'll make amends at the earliest possible moment.'

'Which will be after surgery. Please don't forget, Nurse. It could be important. Even fine modern ships like this sometimes catch fire, or strike hidden rocks and founder. Your life might depend on knowing exactly what to do.'

'Yes, Doctor.' She darted him a scornful look from beneath her lashes which, fortunately, he didn't appear to notice.

Passengers were beginning to hurry past the open surgery door, trailing their life-jackets. For a while there was noise and confusion, and then an almost total silence.They almost certainly wouldn't get any patients until the boat drill was over, Jill reasoned, and she was right.

Five minutes after it ended a woman appeared in the doorway holding a sobbing little girl by the hand. The child still wore her life-jacket which was now liberally sprinkled with drops of blood from a cut lip.

'You wouldn't think she could hurt herself at boat drill, would you?' The mother flung her offspring an exasperated look and handed her over to Jill. 'There we were, all standing meekly on the promenade deck watching them slide back those heavy glass screens and bring down a few of the boats, just to prove they worked, I suppose, and suddenly I noticed Emma was missing. Would you believe it—she'd gone up to the boat deck and tried to climb up into one of the boats they hadn't brought down, if you get me. Only, being Emma, she'd managed to fall and hurt herself.'

David examined the torn lip gently. 'She hasn't broken any of her front teeth and that's the important thing.' He smiled down at the small woebegone face. 'You were a funny girl, Emma, to bite your own lip but it won't look half so bad when Nurse has cleaned it up a bit.'

Jill fetched warm water and cotton wool and removed most of the blood, revealing the extent of the cut. He studied it for a moment and then decided it needed a few stitches.

'Hold her head steady for me, Nurse,' he ordered.

Interested now, Emma behaved perfectly, but apparently the little operation was too much for her mother. Just as they finished the job she slipped to the floor in a faint.

It lasted a very short time. She was soon sitting up again, white-faced and sipping sal volatile.

'Don't expect so much drama every day, Nurse,' David warned when their patients had left. 'You'll probably spend most of your time dishing out pills.'

Jill looked at him thoughtfully as he returned to his magazine. He had seemed quite different during the last twenty minutes and she couldn't fault his handling of the little girl. Maybe, viewed as a doctor, he wasn't so bad.

But nothing would make her change her opinion of him as a man.

Eleven o'clock came and they had had no more patients. Courtesy demanded that Jill should ask permission to leave and she did so curtly, standing stiffly by the desk.

'Yes, of course you may go, Nurse.' He turned a page without glancing up. 'Go and find yourself a comfortable chair. But be careful not to remain too long in the sun. People with your colouring burn very easily.'

'Do you think I don't know that?'

The words had slipped out before she could stop them. Biting her lip, she turned her back and limped painfully to the door. The boat deck was as far as she felt like travelling and she found a chair without difficulty since most of the passengers were either on the promenade deck or higher up. It was delicious to lie there in the sun, her eyes closed, feeling the glorious warmth soaking into her body and knowing that she needn't do any more hobbling about until lunch-time.

It seemed a long, long time since she had risen early that morning, full of excitement, and run lightly up to the top deck to intoxicate herself with beauty to such an extent that she took that crazy risk and slipped.

She was half asleep when a slightly familiar voice suddenly penetrated her dreams. 'Smile, please!'

Jill's eyes flew open. Toni was standing in front of her, his camera in position. As she involuntarily did his bidding he took a quick picture, and then pulled up a chair beside her and sat down.

'The ankle is better?'

Resting it had already had a good effect and she was able to assure him truthfully that it wasn't so painful now.

'Have you been taking photographs all the morning?' she asked.

'Is right.' He leaned his dark head against the back of the chair with his face turned towards her. He was so close that she could see his black lashes were tipped with gold. 'Always I am busy when there is boat drill. The passengers wish to be photographed in their life jackets. Is no matter that they are grotesque, the fat women much fatter and the ugly ones even uglier.'

He sighed and his lean brown fingers lightly touched Jill's. 'If my subjects were like you, how happy I should be.'

'It was a waste of film to take a photograph of me just now,' she told him lazily, ignoring the compliment. 'I don't want my friends at home to see that one ankle is bandaged.'

'I will take many more when you are re-covered. I like better to photograph you in a bikini or sun dress, not that dull uniform. You will not wear it always, I hope?'

'Certainly not in the evenings, but I think I'm supposed to look professional in the daytime, unless I'm going ashore.'

'Then I photograph you when we are at Corfu,' Toni announced.

In his very different way he was as masterful as the doctor, Jill thought with some amusement. But how much more attractively he managed it!

'I shan't go ashore at Corfu unless my ankle is fit enough,' she said regretfully. No need to mention that she had been expressly forbidden to do so.

'You have not been to Greece before?'

'Never. It's always been a dream of mine to visit some of the islands and go to Athens and see the Acropolis.'

'We Greeks are intensely proud of our beautiful heritage,' Toni said emotionally.

If an Englishman had said something like that it would have sounded ridiculous but somehow, coming from the lips of a Greek, it was quite different. Jill said sympathetically, 'I can quite understand that—' and broke off as a figure loomed over them.

It was an overweight middle-aged man in bathing trunks. He was looking reproachfully down at Toni.

'So there you are! I've been looking everywhere for you. The wife wants you to take a photograph of our little party while we're still pale and anaemic-looking, and then another at the end of the cruise when we're all well tanned. Before and After—see?'

'Is my pleasure!' Toni rose gracefully to his feet, winked at Jill behind the passenger's back and followed him up to the next deck.

Alone again, she once more drifted into a delicious state of semi-coma. Lunchtime came far too quickly and she supposed she would have to make the effort to move or remain hungry. Thankfully she remembered that a light buffet lunch was served on the verandah deck which wasn't nearly so far away as the dining room.

She was struggling to her feet when she became aware that she had another visitor. David

Harcourt was towering over her, a walking stick hung over his arm.

'I think you may find this useful,' he said, holding it out with a totally deadpan expression.

It was exactly what Jill had been longing for but she was so surprised that she made no attempt to take it.

'How did you manage to get hold of a walking stick on the ship?'

'I got it from the boutique. They keep a supply because some of the older passengers feel safer ashore if they have the aid of a stick. The Acropolis, for instance, is covered with lumps of marble and they're very slippery indeed.'

'So you bought it.' Jill hesitated. 'You must let me pay for it, of course,' she added awkwardly.

His face darkened. 'I shouldn't dream of it. What do you take me for?'

'But—'

'What an argumentative girl you are!' He thrust the stick at her. 'For goodness' sake take it and stop fussing. If you find it too painful to accept permanently, you can give it back when you've finished with it and I'll keep it for the next idiot who sprains her ankle unnecessarily.'

Jill took the stick from him without another word though there was a great deal she would have liked to say. It would have been nice, for instance, to have felt free to ask him why he should want to spoil what had certainly been a kind thought by such an ungracious attitude afterwards.

There was no doubt that having something to lean on made walking much easier, though it made her feel more conspicuous. As she made her slow way to the verandah deck several people asked her what had happened, and after she had queued at the buffet a young man insisted on carrying her tray for her.

As they shared a table he told her his name was Malcolm Freeman and he was on holiday with his parents.

'I didn't really want to come,' he confessed, gazing at her from beneath a thatch of thick tow-coloured hair. 'But I'm out of work—haven't had a job since I left school, in spite of getting good "A" levels. A guy gets bloody fed up under those circumstances and I knew Dad could well afford to pay all my expenses. He's a successful businessman and doesn't think much of having an unemployed son,' he added bitterly.

'I expect he can't help being disappointed,' Jill suggested diplomatically, 'but he probably understands that it's not your fault.'

'I dunno about that but I don't argue with him because it upsets my mother. She's got heart trouble, you see, and we have to be careful.' He prodded a stuffed vine leaf with his fork. 'Do you know what this is?'

'No, but it's delicious.' Jill had consumed her

own helping with frank enjoyment. 'I'm not at all sure I ought to be eating here,' she confided, 'but it's much easier and nicer than the dining room.'

'Why ever shouldn't you?' he asked in astonishment.

'Because the staff aren't allowed to eat with the passengers as a rule, or go into the posh bars either.'

'What a daft rule! Does it apply to the disco?'

'Oh no, I don't think so.'

'Then I hope you'll come there with me when your ankle is better,' Malcolm said. 'I shall look forward to it.'

They spent the afternoon together, sitting side by side in deck chairs, and Jill felt she had found a friend. The day which had started so disastrously had turned out not so bad after all and her ankle seemed to be improving rapidly.

All the next day she hoped it would be possible to visit Corfu Town, but unfortunately her cautious attempts at exercise only made the ankle ache badly. When, at lunchtime the day after, the ship anchored off the island, she was obliged to admit that she just wasn't up to sightseeing yet.

It was maddening to see the passengers emerging from a great hole on 'D' deck and going off in tenders towards the quay, and Jill soon withdrew to the port side of the ship and immersed herself in a book. From where she sat only the sparkling

Mediterranean could be seen and for a time she forgot the tantalising proximity of land.

But that evening at dusk when the great white ship began almost imperceptibly to move again, she went slowly and carefully up to the top deck—where she hadn't been since her fall—and watched the island gently drifting astern.

It was a magical scene, the colours already muted by the oncoming of night and lights springing up one after another, not only on Corfu but also here and there on the mainland. Above a great black mass of mountains—surprisingly close—there was a young crescent moon suspended in a clear pale sky.

'The mountains of Albania,' said a voice nearby. 'They look very grim, don't they?'

Jill started and half turned. 'Is that Albania? I didn't know.'

She had answered automatically, her mind not at all on what she had said but registering the astonishing presence of David at her side. His voice had been quite different—quiet and gentle—as though even he were affected by the peaceful scene.

'Were you very disappointed at not being able to go ashore?' he asked.

'At the time—yes, but I don't mind so much now because I can still look forward to the moment when I first set foot on Greek soil.'

'You won't have to wait long.' He leaned on the rail, his shoulder just touching hers. 'The Piraeus is our next port—'

'I thought it was Athens,' Jill interrupted.

'Same thing. The port area is called the Piraeus. We shall be there for three or four days and I'm sure you'll be able to do plenty of exploring, provided you promise to be careful with that ankle.'

Jill turned her head quickly. He was bossing her around again and it was on the tip of her tongue to tell him how much she resented it. But before she could speak he put his hands on her shoulders and looked down at her intently.

Perhaps it was the strange eerie light, neither day nor night, but it seemed to her that there was an expression on his face which she had never seen there before, a softness and tenderness of which she had thought him totally incapable.

'I'm sorry I've had to be so autocratic about your sprain, Jill, but it didn't seem to me you'd got much idea of taking care of yourself. I was afraid you'd have a thoroughly frustrating and tiring time at Corfu if I'd let you hobble around.'

She wanted to tell him that there was no question of his 'letting' her do anything, that it was her own commonsense which had dictated she should remain on board. But as she hesitated, very conscious of his nearness and the touch of his hands, the voice of the English hostess came over the tannoy with startling clearness.

'Dr Harcourt, please! Will the doctor go to cabin No 10 on the verandah deck as soon as possible. Calling Dr Harcourt!'

The intimacy which had so strangely enclosed them was instantly shattered. David's hands fell to his sides and his voice immediately became briskly businesslike.

'It seems there's work to be done. I'd better be on my way.'

'Shall I come with you?' Jill asked.

'You can follow slowly in case you're needed. But for God's sake don't try to hurry.'

There was absolutely no doubt about his return to normal behaviour.

CHAPTER THREE

CABIN No 10 was one of the most expensive on the ship and beautifully situated with large windows overlooking open deck. Feeling very strongly that her evening skirt and sleeveless top were most unsuitable for a medical emergency, Jill tapped lightly and entered.

As she did so, a young man standing between her and the bed swung round and exclaimed, 'Hi, Jill!' It was Malcolm Freeman and he looked pale and worried, his thick hair wildly untidy. An older man, partly bald and wearing a well-cut dark suit, glanced at her with a faint suggestion of surprise and then returned his attention to the woman lying on the bed.

'Mrs Freeman collapsed soon after returning from the shore excursion,' David said, his fingers on the patient's pulse. 'It was only a faint, fortunately, but rather a prolonged one.'

Remembering what Malcolm had told her about his mother's heart condition, Jill felt greatly relieved. Nevertheless, Mrs Freeman looked ghastly, with blueish lips and pallid skin, but she was obviously making a great effort to allay the anxiety of her husband and son.

'I don't need all this fuss made of me. I'm perfectly all right now.' Her voice was weak but firm. 'If I just have a good rest—'

'You should never have gone ashore. I knew it would be too much for you. I told you so before we set off—didn't I, Malcolm?'

The boy shrugged and turned away, and David quietly interposed.

'Perhaps you did a little too much walking, Mrs Freeman, and it was certainly rather hot. I prescribe complete rest for the time being and I'll come along in the morning and see how you are. Nurse will stay with you for a little while and make sure you're perfectly comfortable.'

'It's really not necessary—' the patient began.

'For goodness' sake, Netta, do as you're told for once!' Mr Freeman exclaimed. He turned to the doctor. 'You see what she's like—it's extremely difficult to get her to behave sensibly.'

Malcolm muttered something which sounded like, 'For God's sake—' and went out onto the deck. His father stared after him aggressively and then sighed.

'I expect I'd better follow his example. The—er—nurse won't want me getting in her way.' He patted his wife's hand with an air of slight embarrassment. 'If you're ready, Doctor, we can have a chat.'

'I'm just coming. Nurse knows what to do so we'll leave her to get on with it.'

They passed Jill without a glance and the large comfortable cabin suddenly seemed very quiet and empty. Jill went up to the bed and smiled down at her patient.

'I'll help you into a nightie, Mrs Freeman, and sponge your face and hands.' She went into the bathroom to find what she needed and continued talking through the open door. 'Did you enjoy Corfu?'

'Yes, I did and I don't in the least regret going ashore in spite of what my husband said. Poor Gordon fusses so much but I try to make allowances for him. It's hard for him to understand that there are still a few things money can't buy and good health is one of them.'

She lay back against the pillows, panting a little after such a long speech, and Jill—aware that she had allowed too much talking—continued her work in silence. Mrs Freeman did not speak again until she was comfortably settled for the night.

'How did you get to know Malcolm?' she asked sleepily. 'He's got a chip on his shoulder just now and I was afraid he wouldn't make any friends.'

'We met at lunch today and he told me about his—er—present situation.' Anxious not to start a discussion of Malcolm's lack of employment, she hurried on. 'I'm sure you'll have a good night's sleep, Mrs Freeman, but if you have any problems, get your husband to phone the doctor or me, and one of us will come at once.'

Jill closed the door quietly and began to limp slowly along the deck, wondering what to do with what remained of the evening. As she passed the windows of the Verandah Bar she glanced in and saw Mr Freeman in earnest conversation with David. There was no sign of Malcolm and she wondered if he had gone to the disco.

If only she could go too . . . But it was no good moaning about that. She would have plenty more opportunities when her ankle was better.

Sounds of music came from the big lounge and she found an obscure seat at the back from which she could catch occasional glimpses of the floor show. From what she could see, Danielle and the other dancers seemed to be very good. She watched them until the show ended and general dancing began, and then wandered out to the promenade deck.

It was only about ten-thirty and she wasn't at all sleepy. As she hesitated, wondering whether to stay there for a while and read, Toni emerged from a hidden door carrying a huge sheaf of photographs.

'For many, many hours I have slaved in the darkness,' he complained, 'and to what purpose? So that passengers may buy souvenirs of the cruise to take home and show their friends—pictures of themselves burning in the sunshine of the Mediterranean. Ugh! I am nauseated by so many fat women.'

Jill smiled and made no comment, sensing that he was genuinely overtired and in need of a sympathetic ear. Toni continued to make scornful remarks about the majority of his clients and then began to talk about her own photograph.

'Is among these, Jill. Come and help me put them all up on the board and you shall see yours.'

She went with him willingly, glad of his company. Together they fastened several dozen photographs onto a large board placed in a prominent position near the top of the stairs leading below. Studying her own critically, she was glad to see that it had been taken so that her feet were just out of the picture, with no tell-tale bandage visible. Half-smiling, she looked happy and at ease.

'I take another when you are wearing your bikini,' Toni said.

'I told you I must keep my uniform on in the daytime—'

'You would swim in your uniform?'

'I wouldn't swim at all except very early in the morning, and then I would probably go down to the pool in the depths of the ship. It's not used much by the passengers, I believe.'

He gave an exaggerated sigh. 'You have an answer for everything. I think you do not want that I photograph you more intimately.'

There was no reply to that and Jill merely laughed. They began to stroll slowly along the promenade deck until a series of small lights beyond the thick stormproof windows caught her attention.

'What are those? I didn't know we were still near land.'

'There are many islands in this part of the Med, some inhabited, some no more than rocks. It is the lights of houses which you see.'

Toni stopped at an open window and Jill halted at his side. He slipped his arm across her shoulders with a casual, easy gesture. Together they stared out across the dark sea, their heads almost touching.

The air was cool and she shivered in her thin blouse. Immediately his arm tightened and she could feel the comforting warmth of his body, so close to her own. They remained there for several minutes, talking intermittently and watching the winking lights.

Suddenly Jill sensed that someone was standing behind them. She turned round quickly and found David hesitating there, as though uncertain whether to interrupt or not.

'Did you want me?' she asked. 'Mrs Freeman—'

'She's sleeping peacefully. And it's not urgent.'

Toni had not removed his arm from her shoulders but merely turned round too. His head was tilted at an arrogant angle and he exclaimed indignantly, 'Is nearly eleven o'clock. The nurse is off duty.'

'I'm quite aware of the time, thank you,' David snapped. 'The morning will do,' he added curtly to Jill.

'I'd prefer to hear it now,' she said quickly.

'As you wish.' He looked pointedly at the photographer who shrugged his shoulders and moved a few yards away.

'I am not interested in your talk of shop.' Toni hesitated and then seemed to make up his mind. 'Is best I say goodnight, Jill. We meet again tomorrow.'

David stared after him as he began to walk away and then turned to Jill. 'You seem to have a wonderful gift for making friends in a remarkably short time.'

'Is that any concern of yours?' she demanded furiously.

'Er—no, I don't suppose it is.'

'Then I would be glad if you'd refrain from saying things like that.'

Her annoyance seemed to surprise him and he said quietly, 'I wasn't intending to criticise. What I said was a fair comment—or so I thought.'

'Well, I didn't think it was fair. You made it sound as though I'd been going round the ship picking up men. Toni was the first to come to my rescue when I slipped and sprained my ankle.'

'You don't have to explain yourself to me.'

'Of course I don't!' Jill took a deep breath and clung to her temper. 'And now perhaps you'll tell me what you wanted to say.'

'Certainly. I had a talk with Mr Freeman about his wife's condition and he told me she's due for a heart operation as soon as they get back from this cruise. I think the surgeon intends to insert a pacemaker.' He paused and then added stiffly, 'I thought you'd be interested.'

'Naturally I'm interested, but I can't help thinking it was a bit risky to bring her on a sightseeing holiday like this. I would have thought something static, like a quiet English hotel would have been better.'

'No doubt they obtained their doctor's permission.'

'Oh yes, I expect so.' Jill hesitated and then asked, 'Was that all you wanted to tell me?'

'That's all. I said it wasn't urgent.'

'So you did.' She put her chin in the air. 'Goodnight, Dr Harcourt.'

Trying very hard not to limp, she walked towards the top of the stairs. To take her mind off the brief, thoroughly uncomfortable conversation, she began to wonder about the possibilities of going ashore at Athens. The ship would dock, she had been told, at about lunchtime the following day, and the passengers would be taken on a general sightseeing tour of the city by coach.

It didn't sound as though much walking would be involved and she intended to apply for a ticket.

'You won't be able to get one unless there's a spare seat,' Danielle warned her at breakfast. 'Coach tours are for passengers, not the likes of us.'

'What on earth do you want to drive round Athens for?' Helen demanded in genuine astonishment. 'It's much better to go ashore with just a few people and get a taxi. That way you can do what you like—look round the shops or sit outside a café, anything that takes your fancy.'

'I'd like to do that too,' Jill said diplomatically, 'but this is my first visit to Athens and I want to see the sights.'

It irked her to have to ask permission of the doctor before making any plans. They hadn't exactly parted on friendly terms the previous evening. But this morning he was courteous and approachable, and listened to her request with sympathy.

'Of course you can go ashore, but I must warn you that you're likely to be disappointed over the ticket. The coach tour is very popular with passengers.'

'I shall go on hoping anyway,' she told him obstinately. 'Are you staying on board?'

'I am this afternoon. Tomorrow morning I have a trip to make. Officially, of course, I'm supposed to see that you cover for me while I'm away. Would that suit you?'

'Perfectly, thank you.' Jill did her best to match his politeness. 'Have you seen Mrs Freeman this morning?'

'Yes, and I've given her permission to get up this afternoon since she seems none the worse for her attack. There's no question of her going ashore, of course.'

The arrival of a patient complaining of severe indigestion put an end to the conversation. They had several more trivial cases during the hour and a half that the surgery was open and then Jill was free to enjoy the sunshine on deck.

She found Malcolm there, stretched out in a chair, and sat down beside him for a moment. His eyes were closed and his mouth was set in sulky lines but, as he sensed her presence, he looked round and his expression altered.

'It's great to see you, Jill! Just what I needed to cheer me up.'

'Are you worrying about your mother?' she asked gently. 'The doctor says she's doing fine.'

'Actually I wasn't, though I was scared yesterday, of course.' He gave her a half-ashamed smile. 'I was thinking about myself and the hellish afternoon I'm going to have.'

Jill looked at him in astonishment. 'What on earth do you mean?'

'I've got to go on the coach trip round Athens—and with my father too. Mum insists that we don't give it up and it's impossible to upset her by arguing.'

In view of her own desperate longing to be included, it was hard to be kind and understanding of a teenager's problems. Jill didn't even attempt it.

'I reckon you'll live through it,' she told him crisply. 'Why don't you want to go?'

'I'm not interested in ancient remains, and I can't be in my father's company, without Mum to keep the peace, for more than ten minutes without a row.'

'Then I should think it'll be nice for her to have an afternoon on her own.'

Malcolm sat up and leaned forward to get a better look at her. 'What's the matter, Jill? You sounded thoroughly bitchy.'

'Sorry about that!' She bit her lip and forced a smile. 'It's just that I'm envious. I want so very much to get a ticket for the trip and everybody keeps telling me I'm not likely to be successful.'

'You what? Oh, hell!' The force of his reply startled her. 'Why didn't I think of it? You could have had my mother's ticket but it's too late now.

Dad handed it back in case somebody else wanted it.'

'Then perhaps I shall be the lucky one,' Jill said lightly. 'I shall keep my fingers crossed anyway.'

While they were at lunch the *Hellene* was gently nosed into her berth at the dockside. Staring at the port from a vantage point high on the top deck, Jill thought its appearance was industrial and uninteresting. But the Piraeus was the gateway to Athens, she reminded herself. It didn't matter much what it looked like.

Passengers were already pouring ashore down the gangway when she went to see if there was a ticket available. Unfortunately her luck was out.

'I am so sorry, Nurse,' the man from the Purser's office told her, his dark eyes eloquently expressing distress. 'Every coach is full and we already have a waiting list.'

Jill was so disappointed she could easily have cried. It seemed especially hard to bear after not being able to explore Corfu. She turned away disconsolately and, before she had time to adjust her expression, she came upon David pacing slowly along the promenade deck.

'Any luck?' he asked, adding immediately, 'No, I can see you didn't manage to get a ticket.'

'Is it written all over me?' She tried to smile and failed dismally. 'I'm telling myself that it doesn't matter all that much—I shall have other

opportunities—but I'm not being very successful.'

David looked at her thoughtfully and then
stared out of the window at the dreary customs
building below. Beyond it a line of coaches was
already moving off towards the city a few miles
away. He was so obviously debating something
that Jill waited, wondering what was on his
mind.

'Do you remember I told you I have a trip to
make tomorrow?' he asked at last. 'It so happens
that I have an aunt living at Corinth—my
mother's sister who married a Greek—and I
generally visit her when I have the opportunity.
You would be very welcome to come with me
and I can promise you a quick look round Athens
on the way.'

Jill gasped and stared at him in amazement,
but he was keeping his head turned and his
profile told her nothing.

'It's—it's very kind of you but I'm sure your
aunt won't want—'

'She's the soul of hospitality and never minds
an extra guest. Besides, I shall be glad of company on the drive.'

'You're going by car?'

He glanced at her then, as though wondering if
her disappointment had dulled her wits. 'Oh yes,
there wouldn't be time to use public transport. I
hire a car in Athens and drive myself. It's not a

particularly interesting run but I can promise you a glimpse of the Corinth Canal and we might be able to see the old city as well.'

'I'd absolutely love that!' Her face glowed and her eyes were alight with pleasure. 'It really *is* marvellous of you to have thought of it.'

His formal reply was a little chilling. 'Not at all.'

But it was not that which caused Jill's ecstatic expression to change.

'I've just remembered something, Doctor. You asked me to cover for you while you were away from the ship. What about that?'

'We can easily get round it. Nearly all the passengers will have gone off on the outing to the Temple of Poseidon at Cape Sunion. Under those circumstances, it's quite in order for me to tell the Purser we shall both be absent for a time and ask for one of the staff trained in first-aid to be prepared to deal with any emergency which might arise.'

'And Mrs Freeman?'

'Her husband will see that she runs no risks.'

Jill flung her doubts to the winds. 'Then I'd absolutely love to come. The most I'd hoped for in Athens was to see the Acropolis and have a quick look perhaps at a few other places. I never dreamt of getting as far as Corinth. I shall look forward to it tremendously.'

'So shall I,' he said quietly. 'But I want to

make one stipulation before we start out.'

She stared at him in alarm. 'What do you mean?'

'That I should be glad if you'd stop calling me Doctor, except in front of patients. It's quite unnecessarily formal. My name is David and I'd be obliged if you'd use it in future on social occasions, Jill. Is that agreed?'

'Certainly, if that's what you want.'

Her tone was so docile that he looked at her suspiciously. But she kept her lashes lowered and did not let him guess at her thoughts.

CHAPTER FOUR

'There you are,' David said. 'The Acropolis.'

He had halted the car at the roadside and was pointing ahead and upwards. High above, its cold creamy-white marble glittering in the sunshine, Jill saw one of the most famous groups of buildings in the world. An immense gateway, rows of columns, some broken, some miraculously preserved, the remains of numerous other buildings—all scattered over the summit of one of Athens' twin hills.

'It's wonderful! But how on earth did those ancient builders get it all up there?' she marvelled.

'Goodness knows, but they made a good job of it.'

'And created beauty that's lasted for thousands of years.'

'Wait until you see it floodlit. That really is something to write home about.'

A street sweeper, dressed in spotless white and pushing a white-painted basket on wheels, came slowly past and stared at them. He said something which neither could understand but his meaning was clear. They shouldn't have been parking there.

David hastily re-started the car. 'Talking about writing home, have you got a family? You never mention your background.'

Jill repressed a smile. They hadn't, until then, had that sort of conversation. 'My parents are still happily married and I have a brother and two sisters, one a nurse. The family home is near Birmingham and my father is a teacher. I'm afraid we're all terribly ordinary.'

'It's not so ordinary to remain happily married.'

His voice had been sombre and Jill stole a glance at his face, wondering if he was going to be equally forthcoming about his family, and what he would have to tell her. Or perhaps he was married himself and it hadn't turned out well.

He seemed to be giving all his attention to his driving and no doubt it was necessary, since the traffic was thick and fast. Nevertheless, he managed to pause long enough for Jill to stare across the road at a young man wearing a very short white kilt and a cap with a long tassel hanging from it.

'An *evzone*,' he said, 'doing sentry duty outside the old royal palace. He's one of the most photographed men in Athens. Have you brought your camera?'

'I don't possess one,' Jill told him regretfully.

'There's plenty of time for you to get one later. Perhaps your friend the photographer will advise you on the best sort to buy.'

Unwilling to be reminded of last night's annoyance, she did not reply. They were leaving the centre of the city now and turning in a westerly direction along wide straight roads. After a while they came to suburbs and then the beginning of a good motor road.

'How far is it to Corinth?' she asked.

'To the old city, about fifty miles but it won't take long. I think we'd better go there before calling on my aunt.'

The drive was not a very interesting one though they passed an ancient church and monastery which Jill would have liked to pause at. Olive trees, grey and gnarled, grew out of stony ground, and later on there were vineyards which looked green and healthy in the spring sunshine. An old man riding a donkey bare-backed and sitting sideways stared at them briefly as David slowed down for a moment.

'That's the house we shall be visiting.' He waved his hand towards a low white building on a slight rise. 'My Greek uncle owns some of these vineyards we're passing.'

'Have you ever stayed there?'

'Several times when I was at school but not since. I hadn't seen my aunt for years until I took this job as ship's doctor. Since then I've called on her whenever I could manage it.' He changed the subject abruptly. 'I'm going to stop in a minute and we can walk across the bridge over the Corinth Canal. It's interesting because it's such a terrific excavation."

To Jill, staring down and down to a blue streak of water far below, it seemed a little sinister. She was glad she was up above where there was plenty of light and air, and not sailing along at the bottom of those immense concrete cliffs.

They returned to the car and drove on to old Corinth, where David found a space to park.

'I'm afraid you'll find it rough walking, Jill,' he said, 'so please be careful.'

'You needn't worry in case I take risks. I've had enough of being incapacitated.'

It was the first time she had ever visited such an ancient place and she was astonished at how much there was to see. A roadway which had been used by the Romans—still in good condition. The remains of shops which had been there in Biblical times, and a market place which St Paul had known. The whole was backed by a strange flat-topped mountain and glimpses of vivid blue sea.

'It's really super!' Jill stared about her eagerly. 'I've always been absolutely fascinated by old places. I can't thank you enough for bringing me.'

'I'm glad you're enjoying it so much.' He spoke as though he were a little surprised at so much enthusiasm. 'But don't forget Greece is over-stocked with ruins. They get a bit monotonous after a while.'

'It'll be a long time before they reach that stage for me. In fact, I hope they *never* reach it.' Jill looked up at him defiantly, took an incautious step, putting too much weight on her ankle, and stumbled.

David's arms were holding her almost before she realised she had been in danger of doing further damage to herself. Gasping, she found her face pressed against a soft silk shirt as, for a moment, she was off balance and couldn't recover her poise.

'You little idiot—I thought you promised to be careful,' he said softly just above her head.

'There's no harm done—thanks to you.' Hastily she freed herself and stood firmly upon her own two feet.

For some reason she felt quite extraordinarily shaken by the incident. The feel of David's arms about her had been disturbing and she couldn't imagine why this should be so.

Certainly she was liking him a lot better today than at any time during their short acquaintance, but that didn't mean she wanted to get emotionally involved with him.

Jill gave a mental shrug and dismissed the

puzzle of her unaccountable sensations from her mind. Regretfully, she turned her back on the old city as they returned to the car. She wasn't looking forward to the next part of the programme. It still seemed to her that David's aunt would be surprised and perhaps not altogether pleased to have a stranger thrust upon her.

But it wasn't like that at all.

The house was beautifully cool, with black and white tiles, bright rugs and simple Greek furniture. Mrs Papastramou might almost have been Greek herself with her dark eyes, plump figure and black hair. But her voice was reassuringly English and she seemed delighted to see her nephew.

'It's absolutely ages since you were here, David.' She kissed him affectionately. 'I was so thrilled when I got your phone call to say you were coming today.'

'I came in March,' he reminded her. 'Only a month ago.' He turned to Jill, who had been hovering in the background. 'You remember I phoned and told you I was bringing the ship's nurse with me, just for the ride?'

'Oh yes, of course I remember, and I'm sure she's very welcome.' Mrs Papastramou beamed at Jill. 'How are you, dear? It's nice to see you again.'

Jill stared back at her in utter astonishment, momentarily tongue-tied. What could she possibly mean? Bewildered, she glanced at David and found him looking slightly embarrassed.

'This is my *new* nurse, Aunt Stella, and her name's Jill. I'm sorry I introduced her so badly.'

'Oh dear—how stupid of me!' She laughed in genuine amusement, not in the least put out. 'She's rather the same colouring, isn't she? And just for a moment—What was the other one's name?'

'Sonia,' he said shortly.

'Oh yes, of course.' She looked searchingly at Jill. 'There really is a slight likeness or else it's my eyesight. My husband's been telling me I'm getting more and more shortsighted and I'm sure he's right. I shall have to see about getting some glasses the next time I'm in Athens.'

'How is Uncle?' David asked, changing the subject with an air of relief.

'He's very well and extremely busy. I expect he'll be in soon as it's nearly lunchtime. I do hope you and—er—Jill can stay a nice long time.'

He shook his head. 'I'm afraid we'll have to leave immediately after lunch. It's not a good idea for us both to be away from the ship too long.'

'No, I suppose not. Well, you must come again as soon as possible and give me all the news from home. My sister is a shocking correspondent.' She turned to Jill, making an obvious attempt to draw her into the conversation. 'Are you a good letter-writer?'

'Not very.' Jill smiled, trying to throw off the effects of her hostess's unfortunate mistake.

During the rest of the visit she did her best to appear at ease and to join in the talk whenever possible. Mr Papastramou welcomed her politely but found talking in English a strain which plainly irked him when he wanted to relax for a brief while. Jill was glad when the time came to leave.

They drove back to Athens with only spasmodic bursts of conversation. David returned the car to the hire firm and found a taxi to take them to the ship. During the short journey Jill repeated the extravagant thanks she had heaped on him in Corinth.

'I was glad of your company, and as far as I was concerned it was an extra bonus to see how much you enjoyed the trip.' He hesitated, not looking at her. 'I'm sorry my aunt made that silly mistake. It was embarrassing for you.'

Hastily assuring him that it hadn't mattered at all, Jill admitted secretly that she *had* been embarrassed and so had he, though she couldn't think why. The most natural reaction for him would have been to laugh and tease his aunt about her eyesight.

They had reached the dock area and she dismissed the incident from her mind. As they got out of the taxi David told her he was going into the customs building to ring up Mrs Freeman's doctor. He had tried that morning early and failed to get through and he wanted to know the exact details of her case.

'You'd better go aboard and make sure everything's okay,' he instructed.

Jill glanced up involuntarily at the white monster towering above her. Rows and rows of portholes, and above them the windows of the public rooms and the cabins of the more opulent passengers, including the Freemans. The boat deck with its neatly slung lifeboats, and the top deck higher up still, seemed so remote that she could hardly believe they had become, during the last few days, dear and familiar.

Walking up the gangway, Jill thought back to that first day at sea. It seemed ages and ages ago. The introduction to her boss had been unfortunate and she had disliked him intensely. It was really much nicer to have got onto friendly terms with him.

'Is all well on the ship,' the Greek purser told her. 'You have happy time at Corinth?'

'Oh yes, thank you—it was absolutely marvellous.'

Her sparkling eyes told him she was not exaggerating and he beamed at her, delighted to have his homeland so fervently praised.

Deciding that it wasn't worth while changing

into her uniform, Jill went in search of a deck chair. She found Danielle lounging in a sunny corner, surrounded by empty chairs, and joined her.

'The passengers have mostly gone ashore to buy souvenirs,' she murmured sleepily. 'Wouldn't it be wonderful if the ship was always half empty like this?'

'You'd soon be out of a job if it were.'

'As a matter of fact, I've been thinking about looking for a shore job anyway. This sort of life is okay for a time but there comes a moment when you can't stand it any longer. I reckon I'm on the fringe of getting that feeling.'

Jill said nothing for a moment. There was a question she wanted to ask and this seemed to be a possible opening.

'Do people ever leave quite suddenly?' she asked at last. 'I mean, does it sometimes happen that everything boils up inside them and they've just got to get off the ship?'

'It could happen but it's not a good idea to break your contract without some very good reason.' Danielle yawned like a lazy cat and snuggled into her chair.

'I was wondering about my predecessor. Sonia, I mean, of course—not the temporary one. She seems to have left rather abruptly for what was called "urgent personal reasons".'

'It was given out that her mother was ill but—'

'But what?'

'Well, nobody really believed *that*.'

'Why not?'

'Because it was pretty obvious she'd got an entirely different reason for wanting to get away. We all knew she and the doctor had been having an affair and then something seemed to have happened to bring it to a violent end. Sonia *said* he wanted to make it serious and she wasn't keen but I don't know if that was true.' She yawned again and closed her eyes.

It suddenly seemed to Jill that the sun had lost a little of its warmth. Everything around looked the same—the sky was as blue and cloudless and only the smallest of breezes stirred the pennants far above them. The sounds of shore life came faintly and did nothing to disturb their peace.

Yet something had disturbed it, and in her heart she knew quite well what it was.

'What was she like?' she asked abruptly.

'Are you still on about Sonia? I can't think why you're so interested.' Danielle roused herself with an effort and stared at Jill. 'She was a bit like you to look at, only—well, rather specially good-looking.' She floundered a little. 'I don't mean you're not very attractive, Jill, but—'

'I'm not in Sonia's class.'

'None of us were. She was a real blonde, for

one thing, with a super figure and walked like a model. But you're a much nicer person than she was, that's for sure.'

'Thanks,' Jill said with a wry smile.

'It wasn't only that she was such a big-head about her looks, she was so terribly moody. Sometimes she seemed on top of the world and at other times she'd be depressed about nothing. If she hadn't been a nurse I'd have thought she was a bit off her rocker.'

'Nurses aren't any different from anyone else.'

'No? Well, they're supposed to be.'

'Thanks for putting me in the picture anyway. I hadn't realised David was the sort of doctor who goes in for having an affair with his nurse and I'm glad you warned me.'

Danielle looked surprised. 'Aren't you being a bit naive, Jill? I would have thought doctors and nurses having it off together was pretty common.'

'It happens, of course, but I wouldn't have thought it was advisable in the small world of a cruise ship.'

'I'm with you there. As you can probably guess, dancers have a lot to contend with where men are concerned. Male passengers are apt to think we're fair game and some of us are. But not me. Call me old-fashioned if you like but I'm waiting for what our grandmothers' generation called Mr Right.'

Hiding her thoughts behind closed lids, Jill lay back and tried to relax. It was ridiculous to mind about David and Sonia. What had happened before she came on board was no concern of hers. She didn't have to stop *liking* the man just because he'd turned out to be humanly susceptible to feminine attractiveness.

Consequently, when they met in the doorway of the dining room, she accosted him in a friendly manner and asked if he had managed to contact Mrs Freeman's doctor.

'Yes, I got through this time. He wasn't at all surprised that she'd been overdoing it and collapsed as a result. He gave me her full medical history, which could be useful if we have any further trouble.'

'I hope we don't,' Jill said fervently.

'So do I, of course, but it's as well to be prepared.' David hesitated a moment and then swung away to sit down at a table with some of the younger officers.

Feeling oddly unsociable, Jill found a small table and hoped the other seat would remain unoccupied. And yet, when nobody came to join her, she found herself suffering from an equally odd attack of loneliness. She was glad when, after the meal was over, she encountered Malcolm wandering along the promenade deck with his hands in his pockets.

His face brightened when he saw her. 'Come

up to the top deck, Jill, and let's find a secluded corner.'

'Aren't you going in to dinner?'

'Not until the second sitting, and I need somebody to talk to after the boring day I've had.'

'You found Poseidon's Temple boring?' she exclaimed.

'I didn't go to Cape Sunion. Dad decided to stay with Mum and so I opted out too. Instead, I went ashore and mooched around the Piraeus. I found one or two interesting-looking night spots but they were all closed during the day.' He dragged two chairs into the shelter of a glass-walled look-out and sat down.

'I'm glad I met you,' he went on, 'because I've got something to ask you. Tomorrow night, as a kind of finale, there's a visit to some Greek dancing in a garden somewhere in Athens. My mother is mad keen to go, if the doctor will let her, and Dad's got four tickets.'

'You're hoping to take Dr Harcourt with you?'

'Not *him*! I've got something far more interesting to suggest, and it's got the full blessing of my parents, which is a bit rare.'

Jill could well believe it. 'Who then?' she asked as casually as she could.

'Come off it, Jill! You're not as thick as that.' Malcolm smiled and she found herself wishing he would do it more often. 'It's *you* I'm inviting, of course. Would you like to come?'

'I'd love to!' Jill's eyes sparkled. 'But the nurse isn't supposed to join in the passengers' outings unless there's a *spare* ticket.'

'To hell with that. My father asked for four tickets and nobody wanted to know who they were for. But if anybody had he would have assumed his chairman-of-the-board manner and told them loftily that the extra ticket was needed for the nurse in attendance on his wife.'

'That's okay then. I shall look forward to it enormously.'

'So shall I,' he said softly as his fingers found hers and gave her hand a quick squeeze.

Pleased that he was in such a good mood, Jill responded warmly and agreed to go and watch a movie with him when he had had dinner. But the film was an old one and so shortened as to be almost incomprehensible, and neither of them enjoyed it.

They left before the end and Malcolm suggested a visit to the disco. 'If your ankle is up to it, Jill.'

'Not quite, but it soon will be. You go on your own, Malcolm, and I'll be off to bed.'

He had become increasingly affectionate during the film and she was anxious to be rid of him without causing pain. She accepted his good-night kiss and managed to fend off a more intimate embrace before slipping away.

Sleep proved elusive and her thoughts leapt wildly from one subject to another. But though she was genuinely looking forward to the next night, it was the trip to Corinth which occupied her last conscious attention.

It had been such a wonderfully happy occasion—and the first part especially. Before David's aunt made her unfortunate error.

CHAPTER FIVE

'How did you enjoy your evening ashore?' David asked in the morning.

Jill had been obliged to tell him about her invitation, in case he needed her for some emergency. He had wished her a happy time and given every appearance of being delighted she was to have so much pleasure.

'It was wonderful!' she told him enthusiastically, overdoing it a little. 'There was a short drive first and we passed the Acropolis all flood-lit. It was every bit as marvellous as you said it was—like a fairy castle up in the sky. I enjoyed the Greek dancing too and the setting was very romantic. A beautiful garden—'

'I know,' he interrupted. 'I've been there my-self.'

No doubt he took Sonia with him. Jill brushed the thought aside and continued with what she had been going to say.

'But it went on for a very long time and we all got rather cold. I do hope Mrs Freeman won't be any the worse for it.'

'I hope so too,' David said. 'Didn't you take plenty of wraps?'

'Oh yes, and she had her fur coat so I expect she'll be all right.'

It had been an exaggeration to say the whole party had felt the cold, Jill reflected as their first patient arrived. Malcolm's arm round her and his body pressed close to her own had ensured that she was warm if not entirely comfortable. She had done what she could to discourage his attentions but couldn't feel that she had been very successful.

They were busy that morning and during the following day or so. Passengers who had eaten sensibly on the ship had indulged themselves ashore in Athens and also drunk too much ouzo and retsina. The result in many cases was an upset stomach.

To Malcolm's annoyance, he was the one who developed a cold and not his mother. For a few days he was thoroughly disgruntled and only wanted to sit in the sun, soaking up its warmth. Consequently, Jill had no difficulty in arranging to explore Rhodes by herself.

As at Corfu, the ship had anchored some distance from the shore and the passengers were conveyed in tenders. By the time Jill landed, most of them had disappeared and she was able to wander round the old town without constantly seeing familiar faces.

She strolled up the Street of the Knights, explored the ancient Hospital of St John of

Jerusalem, and then toured the numerous souvenir shops, allowing herself occasionally to be tempted into making a purchase. The old town, set inside its massive walls, was unbelievably well-preserved and she could have stayed there for hours if there had been that much time available.

And if she hadn't felt just the least little bit lonely.

Back on board, she stood by the rail watching the last tenders setting out from the quay behind the harbour pillars crowned with twin wrought-iron deer. With the dark mysterious shore of Turkey providing a sinister backcloth it was an exciting and foreign scene which made England seem very far away.

'What did you think of Rhodes?'

David had approached silently and Jill spun round at the sound of his voice.

'It was the best so far, except—' Hastily she swallowed the rest of the sentence. Corinth couldn't really be compared with a magnificent walled city like Rhodes and it was strange that she had enjoyed the first even more than the second. 'I wish we weren't turning back when we leave here,' she finished wistfully.

'What's it matter?' He raised his eyebrows as he looked down at her. 'You'll be coming this way again—lots of times. Besides, there's still Crete to be visited.'

Jill nodded, glad to be reminded, and he continued speaking.

'I stopped by to tell you that there's something on tonight which you won't get again until next year so it shouldn't be missed.'

'Tonight?' Her eyes widened in surprise. 'I don't know what you mean.'

'It's not in the official list of events. I suppose you could say it's a sort of private Greek thing but they don't mind passengers attending. Did you know that tomorrow is Easter Sunday in the Greek Orthodox Church?'

'No, I didn't. Is it different from ours then?'

'Yes, but for goodness sake don't ask me why! Anyway, at midnight, on the top deck, Captain Yannis, with his officers and crew, will celebrate the beginning of this special Sunday. It's very important to them and well worth seeing.'

'You're sure they don't mind spectators?'

'Quite sure. The Greeks aren't like that. The more the merrier is their motto.'

'But what do they *do*?' Jill persisted.

'You'll see. It's not an awful lot actually but it's the atmosphere which counts. It's really terrific. Wrap up well because it's cold up there after dark in April.'

It would have been nice if he'd said, 'I'll see you there,' Jill reflected as she got ready some hours later. For a moment she considered asking Danielle to go with her but she felt instinctively that such an occasion wouldn't appeal to the dancer. And Malcolm probably wouldn't have been interested either, even if he hadn't got a cold.

At about half-past eleven she made her way up to the top deck. It was dimly-lit and very crowded, since quite a lot of the passengers seemed to have heard about it and decided to attend. A small area had been roped off and Captain Yannis, a short swarthy man, stood there behind a table with his officers and some men whom Jill recognised as members of the band.

There were also two small boys holding candles, and some of the passengers had managed to obtain candles too, though none of them were lit. Nothing much seemed to be happening but there was a tremendous sense of expectancy.

Jill found a good position and stood quietly watching. The minutes ticked by surprisingly quickly and when she next looked at her watch she found it was nearly midnight.

'Not long now,' David said at her side.

She started and turned towards him. 'What happens at midnight?'

'You'll see *and* hear.'

A hush had fallen over the chattering passengers. It was as though they all held their breath. And then, exactly at midnight, there was an outburst of such tremendous noise that everyone was startled and began exclaiming in a mixture of languages which were totally inaudible in the uproar.

The ship's siren blared, rockets were let off and went shooting up into the black sky, sending down showers of gold and silver stars, and the candles on the table were ceremonially lit. From these the two boys ignited those nearest to them and the passengers pressed round, lighting their own candles from others.

When the dark scene was well sprinkled with tiny points of light, the members of the band burst out into a loud triumphant song in Greek.

'Well?' David demanded when he could make himself heard again. 'What did you think of it?'

'I wouldn't have missed it for anything.' Radiant, Jill turned towards him. 'Thank you a million times for telling me about it. As you said, the atmosphere is really incredible. Is it all finished now?'

'Oh no—the service goes on for at least three hours. You don't want to stay for that, do you?'

'I wouldn't understand a word and I'm already getting a bit chilly. I'll go down to my cabin as soon as there's room to move.'

They stood back against a small closed bar and allowed the crowd of people to pass slowly by. A few yards away the Captain was declaiming something in a loud voice but the passengers were all behaving as though they had just left an entertainment which had caught their fancy. A man, laughing at something his woman companion had said, pushed past Jill and, without noticing, sent her reeling back against David.

'Sorry! I was afraid he was going to stand on my foot,' she apologised, struggling to regain her balance.

But his arms were holding her close. 'Better stay where you are until there's more room. You mustn't risk hurting your ankle now it's nearly okay again.'

Jill made no attempt to resist. Conscious of his nearness in every fibre of her being, she simply stood there, treasuring the strange inexplicable happiness of the moment and storing it up, to be relived and wondered at in the future.

There were hardly any passers-by now and no reason at all why she and David should remain any longer. Yet he made no move and Jill, firmly imprisoned, had every excuse for leaving the initiative to him.

Suddenly his grip slackened. But instead of being released she was gently turned round to face him. With a swift movement he bent his head and kissed her hard on the mouth.

Jill gasped and looked up into his face. There was a glint of laughter in his eyes and amusement rippled through his voice when he spoke.

'I enjoyed that! So much, in fact, that I'm going to do it again.'

She was ready for it this time, her lips willingly surrendered. Yielding to impulse, she stood on tiptoe and slipped her arms round his neck. This time the kiss lasted for whole minutes and left them both shaken.

David was breathing hard. He rested his cheek on the softness of her bright hair and held her tightly for a moment. She could feel his thudding heart and knew that her own was racing too.

And then, abruptly, she was free. The suddenness of it left her unsteady on her feet but he didn't seem to notice.

He said, in a strange distant sort of voice, 'Time to be on our way, Jill. It's getting very cold.'

But she wasn't cold. Her blood ran hotly in her veins and his ardour had left her face burning. As startled by the sudden change in him as though he had tipped a bucket of cold sea water over her, she turned without a word and led the way below.

She could sense that he was following behind and gradually the tumult of feeling he had roused in her turned to fury. She waited until they had reached the deserted promenade deck and then turned on him.

'Why did you have to do that?'

'Do what?'

Jill raised her eyebrows scornfully. It was perfectly obvious he was playing for time. 'You know perfectly well what I mean.' She hesitated and then rushed on recklessly. 'I know you make a habit of treating your nurses like that but personally I don't think it's a good idea. Besides, it spoilt a very special and completely new experience for me. I—I wish it hadn't happened.'

'I'm sorry about that,' David said curtly. 'I received the impression you enjoyed it as much as I did.'

The truth of his comment stabbed painfully home and Jill felt herself turning pink with annoyance. She hadn't realised she had given herself away as much as that.

'You took me by surprise,' she improvised hastily. 'I wasn't expecting it and—and—'

David finished the sentence for her as she broke off helplessly. 'And you reacted in a perfectly normal and natural manner. So what are you making such a fuss about?'

'It's because you're my boss and I think we should stick to a strictly professional relationship. Things work better that way.'

He was looking down at her thoughtfully and Jill found herself unable to meet his eyes. More and more she was regretting the impulse which had caused her to embark on this conversation. It would have been so much better to have ignored the whole thing.

'You said something about the way I treat my nurses,' he said coldly. 'You've only been on the ship a short while so how can you possibly know anything about that?'

'People talk, you know, on a ship as much as—as in a hospital or anywhere else.'

'I don't doubt it for a moment but I should be interested to know what's being said.'

'I'm sorry. I don't like repeating gossip.'

Listening to herself, she thought how horribly prim she sounded. She wasn't surprised when David exploded.

'I don't care whether you like it or not!' He seized her arm and held it in a grip of steel. 'You can't stand there calmly dropping dark hints and then refuse to explain them. Come on now—' he shook her angrily '—get on with it.'

Jill set her teeth, gathered her strength for a sudden sharp twist, and she was free. She reached the doorway at the top of the stairs and paused for a final attack.

'You can't possibly need to ask me all these questions. You must already know the answers better than most people. And as far as I'm concerned, the subject is now closed. I never want to hear it mentioned again.'

His reply came so swiftly that it reached her before she could turn to flee.

'That makes two of us, Jill. In future we'll do as you yourself suggested and keep our relationship strictly professional.'

Afterwards, lying wakeful in her cabin, she

found the conversation repeating itself endlessly in her head. What on earth had made her start it in the first place? Relentlessly she sought for the reason but when she found it, it did nothing to restore her to a calmer state of mind.

Her anger was not so much at David's behaviour as at her own. That treacherous response to his kisses still had the power to make her burn with shame in view of his abrupt change of mood afterwards.

She had offered herself to him for the taking. Was it any wonder that he had availed himself of the opportunity?

They were both very stiff when they met at the surgery in the morning. Fortunately there were more patients than usual and so they did not have to spend long alone together. As soon as she could Jill escaped and sought the open air.

Taking a short cut through the big lounge she discovered the dancers having a coffee break. Danielle called out to her as she whisked by.

'Hi, Jill—where's the fire?'

'Nowhere, I hope.' Jill laughed and slowed down. 'Did you want me?'

'Yes. Hang on a minute.' Danielle got up with a leisurely grace and sauntered to join her. 'Will you be able to go ashore at Crete?'

'I hope so but I really can't be sure until the last minute.' She hesitated. 'I haven't mentioned it to the doctor yet.'

'Well, try and fix it so you are free in the evening. The dancers have got a night off and as Crete is my favourite island I want to eat at one of the little tavernas along the water front. Will you come?'

'I'd love to! Just you and me?'

'Two girls on their own? You have to be joking! We'd be fair game for every wandering Greek in the place. Actually, it's a party of four, which I think is just the right number. Don't you agree?'

'Depends on who they are,' Jill hedged.

'Of course it does, but our two males are nice boys. One of them is in the purser's office and his name is Spiro. You probably don't know him but I've been out with him once or twice.'

From Danielle's tone it seemed clear that she had paired herself off with the unknown Spiro and Jill immediately asked the all-important question.

'Who's the other one?'

'Toni, the photographer. Everybody knows *him*. Is that okay with you?'

'Oh yes, thanks. I like Toni,' Jill said cheerfully.

'That's fixed then. See you!' Danielle waved her hand and rejoined the other girls.

It did not take the ship long to sail from Rhodes to Crete and they were passing islands for a large part of the time. Gazing at them entranced, Jill thought she would never get used to the infinite variety of them. They were like emeralds set in a sea of sapphire, some small and bare, others large and crowned with the tall spires of cypresses, black against the brilliant sky.

When they reached Crete the ship anchored well out from the shore and the mountainous island lay before them in all its beauty.

'I'm sure you'd like to go ashore,' David said at the end of morning surgery. 'St Nicholas is a very attractive little place.'

'Well, actually—' Jill began briskly to tidy up after the re-dressing of a cut hand, 'I was hoping you'd agree to my being free this evening. I've had an invitation which I'd very much like to accept.'

'An invitation?'

He was looking at her, obviously waiting for more information though she couldn't imagine what right he had to expect it.

'An invitation to eat at one of the tavernas,' she said coolly, telling him as little as possible.

'I see. Certainly you mustn't miss that, unless some major catastrophe occurs.' And, bleakly, he added, 'You'll probably enjoy it very much, particularly if you're with someone who understands the language.'

He was staring down at the desk, his hands idle, and Jill spared a moment to glance at his downbent head. He had sounded depressed and she wondered if he was wishing he also had an interesting trip ashore to look forward to. Maybe, even, that Sonia was there to accompany him?

The day was a peaceful one, with most of the passengers away on the all-day expedition to the ancient Minoan Palace at Knossos. They streamed back to the ship in the late afternoon, tired but apparently in good health, and there were no emergency calls for doctor or nurse.

Jill dressed carefully for the outing, selecting a low-cut sleeveless black top and a flame-coloured skirt. A fleecy shawl which she had bought from an old man on the quay at the Piraeus would provide all the warmth she would be likely to need.

Danielle was in deep madonna blue, her golden curls framing her small face like an outsize halo, and Spiro could scarcely take his eyes off her. He was a slender young man, dark like Toni, and with similar long-lashed black eyes. His English was poor but he and Danielle seemed to understand each other without difficulty.

The tender was full of crew members having an evening off, and for the first time Jill felt herself one of them. They shouted to each other and laughed a lot, and she thought indulgently that they sounded just like a party of children, out to enjoy themselves.

Toni was paying her special attention and she encouraged him recklessly, quite sure that the evening was going to be fun. And so it was—at first.

CHAPTER SIX

'CRETE my home,' Toni announced as the boat approached the quay. 'Is the most beautiful island of all,' he added proudly.

Spiro swung round and made a passionate statement in Greek. Instantly the two men were in the midst of what sounded like a real row.

Danielle watched them with an indulgent smile. 'Don't worry,' she said quietly to Jill. 'They're not likely to come to blows. Greeks get worked up about everything and there's nothing they like so much as an argument, particularly if it happens to be on the subject of national pride or politics.'

'They won't talk about politics this evening, surely,' Jill protested. 'You and I wouldn't be able to contribute anything at all.'

'Goodness—no! Personally I couldn't care less about them.' Danielle sprang lightly onto the quay. 'I'm absolutely starving,' she called back to the two men, who were still totally absorbed in each other. 'Do stop arguing and take us to the place you've picked for our meal.'

They were both instantly at peace and full of

charm. Toni slipped his arm into Jill's as they walked along the quay.

'You like Crete?' he asked.

'This is the first time I've seen it but St Nicholas looks a super little place.'

As they walked towards their taverna she stared round at the pretty little houses and shops, the clean white paint and brilliant patches of colour, roses already in flower among the palm trees and great cascades of purple bougainvillaea.

They crossed a narrow bridge and turned towards the shore. People were sitting at the white-painted tables outside the cafés, drinking aperitifs prior to dining, although it was already nearly nine o'clock.

'We Greeks not like to eat as early as the English do,' Toni said. 'Is childish to dine at seven-thirty.'

'The English don't take two or three hours off in the afternoon,' Danielle pointed out, 'and so they get hungry earlier.'

They came to a taverna which was gay with red and white striped blinds and plants of all kinds tumbling from a balcony. The two men pushed ahead and entered first, leaving the girls to follow.

'Typically Greek,' Danielle commented with an amused glance. 'But I don't care as long as we get fed soon.'

Another tremendous argument had broken out over the choice of table. The waiter was in the thick of it, all three men gesticulating fiercely. But suddenly it was all settled and Spiro and Toni turned round with beaming smiles.

'You come, please. We have good table.'

When they had seated themselves in an alcove, Jill looked round appreciatively. The place was as unlike an English inn as it could possibly be. Strings of onions, peppers and aubergines—real, not plastic—hung from the ceiling. There were wine bottles lying on their sides in racks and the inevitable flowering plants filled every available space. Three guitarists played and sang with passionate intensity.

'Is nice? You like?' Spiro asked.

'Is very nice.' Jill laughed happily. 'And I like it very much.'

Toni was studying the menu and reading aloud from it in Greek. Danielle begged him to translate but this he seemed to find too difficult. In the end the girls left the choosing of the food to their escorts.

The first course was a magnificent and exquisitely arranged dish of *hors d'oeuvres*. This was followed by kebabs of tender steak interspersed with mushrooms and tomatoes, and well-seasoned with herbs. The accompanying items included some of Jill's favourite stuffed vine leaves.

'All I've got room for now is an ice,' Danielle declared.

'Me too,' Jill agreed.

A delicious feeling of something very close to happiness had been steadily creeping over her. They had all been drinking retsina—the girls very moderately, the men a great deal—and although privately she thought it tasted of turpentine, there was no doubt about its stimulating effect.

They sat talking over their coffee for a long time. No one seemed to think they ought to vacate their table, even though the place was very full. The noise was tremendous as human voices rose louder and louder and the musicians struggled to make themselves heard.

Eventually Jill stole a peep at her watch and caught Danielle's eye.

'It's past eleven. Doesn't the ship sail about midnight?'

The dancer nodded. 'These boys are getting a bit out of hand. I reckon we'd better suggest a move.'

She did so at once, backed up by Jill. Immediately there were loud cries of protest. There was plenty of time—why did the girls want to cut short a good evening? Another fifteen minutes passed before they were actually all on their way out to the street.

They had only walked a few yards when a

young man coming from the opposite direction almost collided with the slightly unsteady Toni.

There were expostulations in Greek and then joyous shouts of recognition. Unable to understand what was going on, Jill and Danielle appealed to Spiro, but his English was totally unequal to the occasion.

'Friends,' was all he could tell them, and that they had guessed for thcmselves.

'I hope they won't prolong their reunion,' Jill murmured. 'It's getting late.'

'How do you stop two Greeks in full conversational flight?' Danielle wondered uneasily.

At that moment, to their surprise and consternation, the attitude of the two men changed dramatically. They began to shout at each other in unmistakably angry tones. It was only too clear that an argument had broken out and they were disagreeing violently.

'Come on, Toni.' Jill took him firmly by the arm. 'You haven't got time for a quarrel just now.'

He shook her off with such vigour that she recoiled against the wall. Her shawl had slipped down and there was a sharp pain in her bare shoulder as the rough wall tore at her tender flesh.

She was examining it with some difficulty and fumbling for a handkerchief when a cry of alarm from Danielle jerked her attention back to the two contestants. They were fighting with their fists now, giving blow for blow with sickening thuds.

'Spiro! Do something, can't you? Stop them before they hurt each other,' Danielle begged.

But it was already too late. The newcomer was taller than Toni and had a longer reach. He was also less drunk and therefore his aim was better. Within a few seconds he had dealt such a battery of blows on his adversary's head that Toni's resistance crumbled.

He staggered for a moment, completely off balance, and then fell backwards, hitting his head with considerable force against an iron lamp standard.

White-faced, Danielle clutched at Jill's arm. 'Oh God—what an awful thing to happen! Is he dead?'

'Of course not.' Jill was deliberately matter-of-fact. 'He isn't even knocked out.'

She went down on her knees beside the prostrate form where she was immediately joined by the man who was responsible. Lamentations in Greek filled the air, almost drowning her voice when she spoke quietly to this unexpected patient.

'Don't try to get up for a moment, Toni. Is your head very painful?'

He touched it with his hand and stared stupidly at red-stained fingers. 'Is bleeding.'

'Yes, you've got a nasty cut, but you're not hurt anywhere else, I hope?'

'No,' he agreed after a pause for thought. His fuddled gaze slowly shifted to the other face bending over him and he smiled faintly. 'Okay,' he said weakly. 'You go now.'

The stranger looked at Jill with a question in his eyes and she nodded. 'He's going to be all right. You'd better go.'

He seemed to understand for he scrambled to his feet, looked round cautiously and then fled down the street. His place was immediately taken by Spiro with Danielle behind him.

'Oh, Jill, he looks terrible—what are we going to do?' She stared at the blood-matted hair and shuddered.

'Get him back to the ship as quickly as possible. Can you make Spiro understand that we must have a taxi?'

Spiro had already understood. He nodded and set off purposefully as though he knew exactly where to find transport at that late hour.

'I wonder what they were arguing about,' Danielle said as they waited.

'He from next village,' Toni explained. 'We friends when boys. He say mine a no-good village and headman a fool.' His voice strengthened as some of his indignation returned. 'So we fight,' he finished simply.

It was plain that he had no regrets but the girls

could not share his attitude. They were in a fever of impatience by the time a taxi drew up beside them and Spiro jumped out.

It was a short ride to the quay, and as they drew up the eyes of all four of them turned anxiously towards the water.

The mooring where they had hoped to find a tender was empty. A faint chugging noise in the distance suggested that they had missed it by several minutes.

'*Now* what are we going to do?' Danielle was distraught.

'Can't we get a boat from somewhere?' Jill stared wildly round. 'We've *got* to get back to the ship before she sails.'

The taxi driver had grasped the situation and was sounding his horn. The noise blared out across the bay and seemed to echo back from its curving arms. But there was no alteration in the steady sound of the tender's engine.

The desperate situation seemed to have restored Toni completely. He ran along the edge of the quay, his eyes raking the dark water, and suddenly he started to wave his arms violently.

At the same time they heard a new sound— another marine engine quite close at hand.

'Boat!' Spiro cried excitedly. 'Boat take us to ship!'

There was no time for arguing about the cost. He and Toni emptied their pockets and pressed drachma notes into the boatman's hand. One by one they sprang from the quay into the bobbing little fishing boat, and without wasting a moment they set off towards the distant *Hellene*.

The tender ahead of them was much larger and heavily laden. It proceeded ponderously at a very slow rate of knots. They caught it up with more than a hundred yards still to go and swept past in triumph. There were shouts from the occupants, to which Tony and Spiro replied with spirit, and then they reached the landing stage attached to the ship.

Jill and Danielle stepped out thankfully, immensely relieved to have got back before sailing time after all.

'Thank goodness that's over.' Danielle led the way through the opening onto 'D' deck. 'I'm for bed now, aren't you?'

Jill had halted and was making sure Toni had landed safely. She spoke over her shoulder.

'I can't go to bed until Toni has had some medical attention. He's tough and is making light of it but that cut is quite a bad one.'

'Do you think it ought to be stitched, then?'

'I'm sure of it.' She spoke to the photographer, who was looking at her enquiringly, wondering why she had stopped. 'Come along to the surgery, Toni, and I'll attend to your head.'

'Is nothing,' he said shortly.

'Don't be daft—you must know it ought to

be cleaned with disinfectant, to say the least.'
Jill's tone softened. 'Please be sensible. I know
you're very brave but you can't go around
the ship photographing people with a hole in
your head.'

He put up his hand and felt the gaping cut
gingerly. 'Is awful mess,' he agreed ruefully.
'Hurts too.'

'I'm not surprised.'

Certain now of victory, she took him by the
arm and steered him towards the lift. When they
emerged near the surgery, she took out her key
and unlocked the door. Seen under the bright
lights Toni looked pale and exhausted, and she
made him lie down on the couch.

'Just rest there for a few minutes while I fetch
the doctor.'

'No doctor. Not necessary.' He sat up abruptly
and winced with pain.

'Probably not, but if I don't call him I shall be
in awful trouble tomorrow. I'm sure you
wouldn't want to get me into a row, would
you?'

He lay down again with a sigh which Jill took
for agreement and she sped away down the
corridor to tap on David's door. As she waited
for a reply her heart began to pound with an
emotion which could only be nervousness.

What would his reaction be at this midnight
call? Would he be coolly professional? Or would

he plainly show his disgust because his nurse had been involved in a brawl between two drunken Greeks?

The door opened suddenly and David stood there wearing dark blue pyjamas edged with white, his hair on end. He stared at her in amazement and then noticed her grazed shoulder.

'You're hurt! What on earth's been happening?'

Jill had completely forgotten her own injury and she now dismissed it cursorily. 'I wouldn't have disturbed you for a trivial thing like that. The person who needs your attention is Toni, the photographer.' Briefly she explained what had happened, saying as little as possible about the amount of retsina which had been drunk.

'I'll put some clothes on and come along at once. Go and stay with him, Jill, and make him keep quiet. He's probably got concussion.'

Jill repressed a smile as she turned away. Toni hadn't exactly been kept quiet during the hazardous return to the ship and she had been powerless to restrain him.

Back in the surgery, she slipped a plastic apron over her evening blouse and skirt and scrubbed her hands thoroughly. She was busy collecting what was needed for attending to the wound when David arrived. He went straight to the couch and made a gentle examination.

'If you want to have a nice neat scar which will easily be hidden by your hair, this will have to be stitched. But first I'm going to cut away a little of this thick thatch. We can't have hairs getting mixed up with the stitches.'

Toni looked alarmed but seemed too weary to protest. When they had finished cleaning and drawing the cut together, he sat up rather shakily and swung his legs to the floor.

'Can go now?'

David looked at him thoughtfully. 'Where's your cabin?'

'Down—down—near bottom of ship. Photographer not important.'

'Then I think you'd better stay here for the night, just in case you start showing signs of concussion.'

'No!' Toni exploded. 'Not necessary.'

'I consider it *is* necessary. Nurse will settle you comfortably and one of us will look in early in the morning to see how you are.'

The photographer hesitated and then his white face was suddenly adorned with a beaming smile. 'Nurse will settle me? I like that! Shall sleep well when she has—how you say it? Tucked me up?'

Jill laughed but caught no answering gleam of amusement in David's face. He was looking quite extraordinarily grim considering that he had won his point without much difficulty.

She went into the miniature hospital, where the three beds were always in readiness, and turned down the nearest one. There was a towelling dressing-gown in one of the cupboards and she fetched it and handed it to Toni.

'Sorry we can't supply you with pyjamas but you can sleep in your underwear for tonight.'

'Someone will fetch what you want in the morning,' David told him.

Toni was horrified. 'Not want pyjamas then! Must start work after breakfast.'

'I really must insist on your spending at least one day in bed after a knock like that.'

'No—will not!' It was almost a shout and there were signs of increasing agitation.

'You really *will* get concussion if you work yourself up like that,' Jill said quickly. 'Calm down, for goodness' sake, and let the morning take care of itself.'

Toni looked mutinous and then subsided with a sigh. 'Am calm now.' Meekly, he disappeared into the next room and began to undress.

'You seem to know how to handle him,' David said stiffly.

She glanced at his set face and shrugged. 'It's not very difficult. I've been handling awkward patients since I was eighteen.'

As she tidied the surgery and washed her hands again, she wished David would go away. He was fidgeting about, doing nothing in particu-

lar, and then—just as Toni called her—he made
a definite move towards the door into the corridor.

Relieved, Jill went into the hospital and found
her patient lying flat in the neat white bed. He
looked desperately tired and somehow much
younger than usual. She tucked him in carefully
and smoothed the bedspread. When she had
finished he caught at her hand.

'Is nice to have you to look after me, Jill.'

She smiled. 'It would be much better not to
need looking after.'

'Georges insult my village and so I knock him
down.'

She did not point out that he was the one who
had been knocked down. No doubt he had
already rewritten the incident in his mind and
was satisfied with the result.

As she bent over him he pursed his lips into the
shape of a kiss, looking up at her appealingly.
With almost no hesitation and a tenderness that
was entirely maternal, Jill bent her head and
kissed him lightly on the forehead.

'Thank you for a wonderful evening,' she said
softly. 'I enjoyed it enormously right up to the
last bit.'

She was quite unprepared for the intensity of
his reaction. His arms snatched at her fiercely
and his wine-laden breath was hot on her lips. As
she struggled ineffectually his mouth clung to

hers with a passion which aroused in her no vestige of response.

Perhaps Toni realised her lack of co-operation for he released her abruptly. With a slightly rueful smile he closed his eyes and prepared for sleep.

Jill straightened herself and turned round. David was standing in the doorway, his expression icy.

'Sorry to interrupt,' he said curtly. 'I just wanted to remind you to lock up.'

CHAPTER SEVEN

FURIOUS because she knew her colour had deepened, Jill answered with equal curtness.

'Do you think I'm likely to forget? I'm not as irresponsible as that, I hope. Besides, it was my key which was used to unlock the surgery so of course I shall remember.'

David seemed surprised at the indignation in her voice. 'It's easy to forget when—'

'When what?' she asked coldly.

He turned back into the other room without answering. Jill switched off the light, reminded Toni that he had a bell handy in case of need, and also a telephone, and said a cool goodnight.

'Since you apparently can't trust me, you'd better supervise my locking up,' she said as she picked up her bag and crossed to the door.

'Don't be like that, Jill.' David sounded thoroughly exasperated. 'You know darned well the circumstances warranted my taking precautions.'

'And what's that supposed to mean?' she demanded angrily.

He shrugged. 'I don't think it's really necessary for me to answer that.'

Afraid of losing her temper completely within earshot of the patient, Jill locked the surgery and stormed down the corridor to her cabin. She had opened the door and was about to disappear inside when David caught her up.

'I've got to say this, Jill, even if you hate me for it. It's not a good idea to let yourself get involved in quarrels ashore between Greeks. They're a very hot-blooded lot and anything could happen. As ship's doctor, I feel responsible for your safety.'

Jill whirled round furiously. 'Will you kindly stop interfering in my life? I'm perfectly capable of looking after myself and what I do in my free time is my own affair. I like Toni and—'

'That's obvious.'

'So what? Any reason why I shouldn't?'

'A very good one. You haven't been on the ship long enough to be able to cope with the peculiar effects of shipboard life. In a way you're cut off from the world on a ship and everything is abnormal or exaggerated. If you're not used to it you're apt to think emotions are for real when in reality they're superficial and not to be taken seriously.'

Jill stamped her foot. She couldn't remember when anyone had made her so angry.

'Thanks for the lecture!' she flung at him. 'I suppose you think I ought to be grateful? Well, I'm not! It's an absolute insult to tell me I don't know how to distinguish between real life and what happens on a cruise. I've been around, you know—I'm not a starry-eyed student nurse in her first year.'

Backing away from him she would have closed the door in his face if he had not taken a swift step forward and blocked the doorway.

'For God's sake, Jill—keep your voice down. It's very late and we shall have the passengers complaining of being disturbed.'

'I don't care!' She stood staring at him, her breast rising and falling with quick breaths of anger.

But suddenly her eyes dilated and she took another involuntary step backward.

'Oh, my dear—' David stepped inside the cabin. 'I can't leave you like this. I've got to get it sorted out somehow. Please, couldn't we just talk quietly for a few minutes?'

And he closed the door behind him.

They stood looking at each other for a moment and it seemed to Jill that he must hear her heart thudding plainly in the silence of the cabin.

At last she found her voice. 'I don't understand. What is there to talk about? I would have thought you'd said quite enough already.'

'I said all the wrong things.' David was looking white and strained, his grey eyes full of distress. 'I meant well but I made a terrible mess of it.'

'It's hard for me to believe you meant well. It

seemed like the most unwarranted interference in my private life.'

'I'm sorry but I was so afraid you'd get hurt.'

'By Toni?' Somehow she managed a scornful laugh. 'I'm in no danger of that. Did you think we were having an affair and I might take him seriously? I've only known him about ten days.'

'Time has nothing to do with it, especially on a ship, and—and when I saw you saying good-night to him—'

'You jumped to a perfectly ridiculous conclusion.'

'I'm relieved to hear you call it ridiculous,' David told her, all the previous stiffness back in his voice.

'Good. And now perhaps you'll go away and let me get to bed.'

'Yes, I'd better do that, I suppose.'

But he still lingered, his head downbent. There was something else he wanted to say, Jill was sure of it, but she could not imagine what it was.

When he finally made up his mind to tell her, the shock was so great that she was completely speechless.

'Jill—' He had raised his head and was looking straight at her. 'Will you forgive me for being such a blundering idiot? I had a good reason for what I said but it wasn't any of the lofty reasons I've been handing out—not that they weren't mixed up in it too, of course,' he added wildly.

For a long moment he held her gaze and then she asked in bewilderment, 'Aren't you going to tell me what it was?'

'I was jealous,' he said simply. 'When I saw that bloke kissing you I would have knocked his block off if he hadn't been my patient.'

Jill gasped and then tried to laugh. 'As his medical attendant you'd have been behaving disgracefully.'

'I've just said that was the only thing which stopped me.'

'I—I still don't see why you minded.'

'It's simple enough. If there's going to be any kissing going on around you I want to be the one who's doing it. Maybe it's a primitive urge, going back to caveman days, but I can't help that.'

Her pulses were racing even faster now but somehow she managed to speak lightly.

'Has nobody ever told you caveman emotions aren't fashionable any longer? It's ridiculous to feel that way about anybody like Toni. He's got as much right to kiss me as—as anybody else, and it means just as little.'

There was a long silence before David answered her. Jill could plainly hear her own breathing and his too but there was no other sound. The ship ploughed steadily on, with no perceptible motion, carrying her sleeping passengers towards another long, sunny day. For a moment Jill had the fanciful notion that—apart from the officers on watch—she and David were the only people awake in the whole vessel.

He said abruptly, his eyes boring into hers, 'That time I kissed you on the top deck, after the Easter ceremony, was that as unimportant as you're making out? It seemed to me then that it was for real.'

'I guess we were both a bit carried away by— by the occasion.' She wrenched her gaze away from his and shrugged. 'Looking at it with hindsight I can see it was just a typical shipboard embrace.'

'I got the impression that you enjoyed it.'

'So I did in a way,' Jill said carelessly. 'I was glad to wipe out the memory of that first day when you treated me just like I was a child.'

It was a feeble explanation, as she well knew, but David appeared to accept it.

'I thought you were a complete idiot then,' he admitted. 'It wasn't until we went to Corinth that I began to change my mind about you. Since then I've changed it quite a lot more. Jill—' with a swift movement he put his hands on her shoulders so that she was a prisoner '—I know you think I'm bossy and interfering but I do really *mind* what happens to you, you know. It's important to me that you shouldn't do daft things like you did tonight in Crete.'

'So we're back to that, are we?' she demanded

angrily. 'I thought I'd made it plain that I don't exactly make a habit of getting embroiled with quarrelsome Greeks and, in any case, how I behave when I'm off duty is no concern of yours.'

'For goodness' sake don't start that again!' As furious as she was, he shook her violently.

'You began it—not me.' As she struggled to release herself his grip tightened.

David's mood changed abruptly. 'We're a couple of fools, Jill, to let ourselves get worked up like this. There's only one cure that I know of and I'm going to try it whether you like it or not.'

'What is it?' she demanded.

'I'm going to repeat the experience of the top deck.'

His hands slid down from her shoulders and began to caress the soft flesh beneath her thin blouse. A shiver of sensuous delight passed over her and when he bent his head to capture her lips she surrendered willingly, giving herself up to the rapture of the moment.

She did not even protest when he drew her down on the bed and they lay there in each other's arms, their hearts beating with equal fierceness and their bodies urgent with longing for total fulfilment.

David was the first to move. With a suddenness which startled Jill, he sat up and swung his legs to the floor.

'Afraid I got a bit carried away, love.' He was

breathing hard. 'Sorry about that. You shouldn't be so attractive.'

With a haste which matched his own, Jill also stood up. 'We're not going to start arguing again, are we?' she asked tartly.

'I hope not.' He looked at his watch. 'It's far too late for rational thought and we'd both better get what sleep we can. See you in the morning.'

She made no reply but as the cabin door closed behind him softly she collapsed again onto the bed and lay there, staring up at the ceiling.

David's abrupt departure had left her feeling utterly sordid. It seemed to her in that bleak moment that he had used her merely as a partner in a pleasurable exchange of caresses which meant nothing more than physical enjoyment. Surely, if the incident had been of the slightest importance to him, he wouldn't have gone off without some show of tenderness?

As for herself, the intensity of her feelings while they lay together on the bed had frightened her badly. She had never believed in making love in the fullest sense with anybody who happened to attract her, but she had longed passionately to make love with David. Did that mean she loved him?

It seemed a naive assumption and one she certainly wasn't prepared to make. Besides, nothing he had said had given the impression that he had any feelings for her except the normal ones of a virile male.

If Danielle was to be believed, even Sonia had had more from him than that.

Too much had happened during the last few hours and reaction was setting in fast. Jill gave up the unequal struggle with the tears which threatened to overwhelm her and let them flow freely. By the time the torrent ceased her eyes were swollen and her head ached but emotionally she had found relief. Just as she was, still dressed, she fell into a deep sleep.

Hours later she woke up, freezing cold. In a daze she pulled off her clothes and got into bed properly, almost immediately subsiding again into the healing depths of total forgetfulness.

It was inevitable that she should sleep late and when she eventually struggled back to consciousness she discovered it was half-past eight. There was no time to relive the events of the night, even if she had wanted to, and she got up at once and took a quick shower.

As she dried herself afterwards, she suddenly remembered Toni.

He would think she was never going to release him from imprisonment. Unless, of course, he was still asleep. As he hadn't rung the bell to summon her, she was inclined to think that he was.

She assumed her guess was correct when she

unlocked the surgery door a little later and got no reply to her greeting. With quiet steps she went across to the open door of the tiny hospital and looked in.

Toni's bed was empty.

For a moment Jill stared stupidly. He must be in the toilet annexe—yes, of course, that was the solution. He couldn't just have vanished into thin air.

She waited for a few seconds and then called out again. 'Toni—are you all right?'

There was no reply. Seriously concerned now, Jill made a thorough search of the annexe, but there was no sign that anyone had used it. The towels were neatly folded, the soap still dry.

Surely she *had* locked the door properly last night?

Convinced that she had, Jill locked it again and turned in the direction of David's cabin.

She met him almost at once, walking towards her, and at the sight her heart gave a sickening lurch and all her concern for Toni was momentarily swamped by the memory of last night. She went eagerly to meet him but almost instantly her smile of greeting was killed by the thunderous expression on his face.

He said angrily, 'What have you done with your photographer friend? Surely you haven't been crazy enough to let him get up? You *must* know that someone suffering from concussion needs to stay in bed and keep quiet?'

Hurt and bewildered, Jill leapt to her own defence. 'Of course I know that! What do you take me for? I haven't done anything with Toni. He's simply disappeared.'

'It's impossible!' David snapped. 'I know you locked the door because I watched you. I could hardly believe it when I found him missing this morning and, naturally, I assumed you'd gone in earlier and given him permission to get up.'

'I wouldn't dream of doing that without asking you first.'

He looked down at her, his brows still drawn into a straight line and no sign of softening in his face. 'I don't suppose you'd actually intend to, but I wouldn't mind betting that bloke could be pretty persuasive if he set himself out to get round you.'

'Oh yes, Toni's certainly a charmer,' Jill agreed with considerably more fervour than was necessary, 'but if you believe I'd let him influence me on a professional matter, then I think you're being downright insulting.'

'Sorry,' he said curtly. 'I'm afraid I'm not in a very good mood this morning.'

He was avoiding her eyes now and, as she gazed up at him in pain and perplexity, she tried to make sense of this totally unexpected attitude towards her. Finding no clue in his face, she was obliged to fall back on an acid reply.

'That's only too obvious, David.' She waited a moment but, as he said nothing, she dared to add, 'What on earth's the matter with you?'

'Call it a hangover if you like.' He smiled grimly. 'But not in the usual sense, of course. I owe you an apology, Jill, for last night. I came pretty near to getting completely carried away but I never intended it. You've got to believe that.'

Jill's eyes widened in dismay. She didn't want an apology. She had been hoping for tenderness and perhaps even some sign of love; she had certainly never expected this bitter regret, in spite of his abrupt departure from her cabin.

'I think you're exaggerating to an absurd degree,' she said crisply. 'It would be far better to forget all about it—as I intend to do. And now, for goodness' sake, let's decide what should be done about Toni. That's far more important.'

To her relief David visibly relaxed. He touched her bare arm lightly with his fingers, sending a tremor all the way to her heart.

'Thanks, Jill—and don't worry about your friend. I'll go and report the mystery to the Staff Captain. There's probably quite a simple explanation.'

'I can't imagine what it is.'

'Nor can I but we'll soon find out. Go and get some breakfast while I see to it.'

She was too puzzled and distressed to feel hungry but she made her way to the dining room and ordered orange juice from a reproachful steward.

'Is late, Nurse,' he reminded her.

'Yes, I know. I slept too long.' She smiled at him and received a forgiving smile in response.

Passengers were already streaming into breakfast and she saw Malcolm's father sitting at a small table by himself. On her way out a little later she paused to ask about his wife.

'Netta seems fairly well, thank you, Nurse,' he told her, his heavy face careworn and unsmiling, 'but I'm not sure it was a good idea to come on this cruise.'

'Because it's so difficult to persuade Mrs Freeman to rest?'

'Exactly. It would be all right if we spent all our time at sea but she hates not being able to go sightseeing. She's very energetic by nature. Quite different from Malcolm,' he added bitterly.

'I'm sure she must find it very frustrating. Is she to have the pace-maker fitted soon after she gets back?'

'The following week. I've booked her into a private clinic.'

'Then there's not long to wait. We shall be at

Venice in a couple of days,' Jill reminded him in the voice she used for soothing nervous patients and their families.

'Do you know how long the ship spends at Venice before sailing with a fresh load of passengers?' he asked, looking at her thoughtfully.

Surprised at the question, she was unable to give a definite answer. 'I think it must be quite a while. They'd need to stock up with provisions and all that. Would you like me to find out for you?'

'Thank you, but I can easily do that myself. We're at the Captain's table for dinner and I'll ask him tonight.' Mr Freeman waved his hand at the chair opposite. 'Sit down, Nurse, and I'll tell you why I want to know.'

She took the empty seat and looked at him expectantly, quite unable to guess why he should be interested in the *Hellene*'s programme after he and his family had left the ship.

The explanation was a considerable shock to her.

'Flying isn't generally considered a good thing for people with heart trouble,' he began. 'Isn't that right?'

'Well, yes, but—'

'You're going to point out that plenty of them fly in perfect safety. Yes, I know that, but it doesn't stop me worrying about my wife, especially after the fright she gave us at Corfu.' He leaned his arms on the table and looked earnestly at Jill. 'I would be very grateful if you could fly back to Gatwick with us and keep a professional eye on Netta. I would be responsible for all your expenses, naturally.'

For a moment Jill was too surprised to speak. When she had recovered sufficiently to find her voice, she said doubtfully, 'But won't the plane already be full?'

'We didn't come on the charter flight. I feel fairly confident I can find a seat for you on the ordinary flight with us. Anyway, I'm sure something can be arranged.'

No doubt it could, Jill thought wryly. When you had the sort of money that Gordon Freeman obviously possessed you could accomplish almost anything.

'Of course I'll come,' she promised readily, 'provided there's enough time. But I shall have to ask the doctor's permission,' she added as an afterthought.

'I don't anticipate any difficulty there. Harcourt is a thoroughly reasonable chap.'

Not trusting herself to comment on that, Jill took her leave. Owing to her late awakening it was nearly surgery time but she decided she could just fit in a quick visit to the open air to look at the weather. The worst of having an inside cabin was being without a porthole, and the dining room was also windowless, so, for all she knew, it could be raining outside.

But sea and sky were both as blue as ever, with only the smallest and whitest of clouds occasionally drifting by. Trying to shake off her depression, Jill stood by the rail, absorbing the warmth of the sun and wishing that David's moods were as dependable as the weather.

Turning away reluctantly to go below, she saw Toni coming towards her.

CHAPTER EIGHT

JILL stopped abruptly, looking anxiously at the photographer and noting a slight pallor but nothing more. He had combed his thick dark hair over the stitches and they were invisible.

'How are you feeling, Toni?'

'Okay,' he answered with a shrug.

'How on earth did you get out?'

He gave her a slow complacent smile. 'Is simple. I phoned Spiro to tell him I am prisoner. He brought master key and unlocked door.'

It was impossible not to give him an answering smile though she tried to scold him as well. 'You should have stayed in bed until the doctor had seen you. He's very angry with you.'

'No need to stay in bed.'

'But haven't you even got a headache?'

He shrugged again. 'Perhaps, but is not important.'

'It might be—'

But he was already on his way to start the day's work. Continuing in the opposite direction, Jill reminded herself that he had probably taken part in many similar fights in the past, though perhaps not to the extent of requiring stitches.

He doubtless regarded the incident as a normal part of life.

David had already unlocked the surgery when she arrived. He was brisk and businesslike and seemed to have forgotten his former bad temper.

'I found out how Toni escaped,' he told her.

'So did I. I met him out with his camera as usual.'

'He doesn't realise the risk he's running and I expect he'll get away with it, too.'

'I hope so,' she said levelly.

His eyes were on her face but all he said was, 'I hope the same, naturally.'

They were busy that morning, with few intervals between patients, but at the end of the session Jill remembered her conversation with Mr Freeman. David listened without interruption as she told him about the request which had been made to her.

'Do you think it's practicable for me to go?' she finished.

'Practicable, I suppose, but hardly necessary. If Mrs Freeman behaves sensibly and remembers to take her tablets she should be perfectly all right.'

'Yes, I know, but he does seem very worried and I more or less promised to go, provided I had your permission.'

'I see no reason for withholding it—except

one.' He came closer, setting her pulses racing. 'And that's entirely personal. I thought you might like to look round Venice while the ship is in dock. We could have fitted in a little sight-seeing and then had dinner somewhere. I know several good places. There might even have been time for a trip in a gondola. Would you have liked that?'

'Oh *yes*—it would have been wonderful.' She looked at him with more of her heart in her eyes than she would have wished to show.

He sighed and absently twisted a tendril of copper-bright hair round his fingers. 'I would have enjoyed it too but I'm afraid you must go with the Freemans to Gatwick.'

Jill's whole face spoke eloquently of her bitter disappointment. 'I do wish they hadn't asked me—'

'So do I, but you'll have to accompany them because, if you didn't and Mrs Freeman had a heart attack, neither of us would ever forgive ourselves.'

'That's true,' she agreed despondently, and then suddenly brightened. 'Perhaps I shall be back in time to go into Venice after all? It's such a short flight.'

But David shook his head. 'The ship will sail about ten o'clock, I expect, and we'd need to start out quite early to fulfil that sort of pro-gramme. It would spoil it to rush things.'

'Yes, I expect it would. Oh well—it will be something to look forward to next time we are at Venice.'

Afterwards she wished she hadn't said that. David had not mentioned anything about the outing being only postponed. She had simply assumed it. As she went in search of the Freemans, she had an uneasy feeling that her own disappointment had grcatly exceeded his.

Perhaps it was because he had probably been to Venice several times, whereas for her it would be the first time.

Perhaps he had taken Sonia there.

She found Netta and Gordon Freeman in a quiet corner of the boat deck, their heads in the shade, and lost no time in imparting her news.

'Thank goodness for that!' he said fervently. 'I'm very grateful to you, Nurse.'

'I'm sure it's not necessary,' his wife complained. She smiled at Jill. 'But I shall love to have your company and I know Malcolm will too. I hope we haven't upset any plans of your own?'

'Oh no.' The denial sprang easily and convincingly to Jill's lips. 'I like flying and I'm quite happy about the arrangement.'

'Just one thing,' Netta called after her as she was moving away. 'Don't wear your uniform, dear. It would make me feel so conspicuously an invalid. You won't mind?'

'Goodness, no! I shall be much more comfortable in jeans and a tee-shirt.'

They reached Venice the following morning. Resigned now, Jill got ready in good time and went ashore with the Freeman family.

'Long time no see!' Malcolm greeted her.

'Not my fault,' she told him. 'You've been nursing your cold and thoroughly unapproachable.'

'I didn't want to give it to you.'

'Don't you know nurses never catch things? We develop immunity over the years.'

'Really? Then there's no reason why I shouldn't do this.' And he kissed her enthusiastically in the doorway of the customs shed.

His father gave a snort of disgust. 'Must you make an exhibition of yourself? Come and help with the luggage, for goodness' sake.'

Jill retired with Netta to a comparatively quiet corner, where they waited for the customs formalities to be concluded. As she watched the sun-tanned passengers of the *Hellene* wrestling with suitcases, Jill thoroughly appreciated her own unencumbered state.

By tonight these unfortunates would presumably be back in their own homes, their cruise already a thing of the past, but it would be different for her. *She* was coming back to the ship—and to David.

Her eyes grew dreamy as she thought again

about that scene in her cabin. She had been badly upset by the way he had spoken to her the following morning but she had got over it now. They hadn't known each other very long and perhaps things had been going a bit too fast. It would be better to slow down and let their love grow and develop gradually.

Their love? Jill bit her lip so savagely that she almost made it bleed. David had never said a word about loving her, though he had made it plain that he was attracted, which wasn't the same thing at all.

'Thank God that's over.' Mr Freeman appeared in front of them. 'Come on, let's go and sit in the launch.'

Jill jerked herself back to her surroundings and resumed her duties. There was Malcolm to be handled tactfully and his mother to keep an eye on, and she mustn't let her mind wander.

Neither task proved onerous. Malcolm was more cheerful than she had ever seen him—perhaps he was relieved that the cruise was over—and Netta gave no cause for alarm. The long trip across the lagoon was uneventful, and the flight was easy and pleasant.

At Gatwick Jill joyfully accepted her return ticket to Venice and shrugged off the profuse thanks of both the elder Freemans.

'I shall miss you,' Malcolm said.

She didn't believe him but all she said was,

'You'll soon get re-absorbed into your normal life, and you'll probably get a job before long. Your luck's got to turn some time.'

'I don't see why,' he told her with a return of his customary gloom.

With all her heart Jill hoped he would be successful, but inevitably as she waited for her flight to be called her thoughts left the Freeman family and flew ahead to her own immediate future.

Fortunately nothing delayed her return to the *Hellene* and the flight was as uneventful as the previous one. At least it seemed so to Jill, and no sixth sense warned her that things were not exactly what they seemed.

Lost in dreams, she took little notice of her fellow passengers. She did not even take any interest in the girl sitting next to her until the stewardess started to bring round the usual plastic trays laden with odd scraps of plastic-looking food.

'I'll have a glass of red wine,' the girl said as she received her tray. And to Jill she added, 'It helps to make this stuff a little more edible, don't you think?'

'I expect it does, but I'm quite hungry actually and consequently not all that critical.' Jill smiled, vaguely aware of slim legs in scarlet trousers, shoulder length fair hair with a slight wave at the ends, and a quick impatient voice.

'Thank goodness for some blue sky.' The blonde was staring out of the window, her face hidden by a curtain of shining hair. 'It's been hellish cold in London lately, hasn't it?'

'Oh—er—has it?' Not bothering to elaborate and admit that she knew little about the recent English weather, she asked if the girl was going on holiday.

'I'm taking a cruise and I can't wait to feel some warmth on me. If I'd stayed in England any longer I would have lost my tan completely.'

'However did you manage to acquire a tan in England at this time of the year? Sun lamps?'

The hair was tossed back and she glimpsed a faint smile. 'I've only been enduring the English climate for the last month. Before that I was in the Bahamas.'

She went on talking in a quick, rather high voice, her words tumbling over each other, describing the lazy, colourful life in the Bahamas and how much she had enjoyed it.

'Seems a pity to have left it,' Jill said, since some comment was obviously expected of her.

'I didn't have any choice—my job came to an end. Well—sort of.' For the first time there was some slight hesitation. 'Anyway, everything's going to be okay now.'

Bewildered, and not particularly interested, Jill asked if she was going on holiday all alone.

'Oh no, I'm meeting my fiancé.' She turned her head towards Jill, revealing a pair of brilliant blue eyes which sparkled like sapphires.

There was something slightly disturbing about those eyes. Their brilliance seemed unnatural, as if they were lit by a burning intensity of feeling in the brain behind them. A little uneasy, Jill averted her gaze and tried to let the conversation lapse.

But the girl continued talking non-stop until they began to circle the airport at Venice. There was nothing much in what she said and, afterwards, Jill could hardly recall any of it. She was glad when the plane door was opened and she could escape.

Ahead of her as she crossed towards the customs building a heavily pregnant young woman was walking slowly. Was she going to be one of the *Hellene*'s new passengers? Looking at her with a professional eye, Jill hoped the birth of the baby wasn't as imminent as it appeared.

Taking her place in the launch she was glad to see that her previous travelling companion was seated some distance away. Somehow—though she couldn't have given a reason—she hadn't liked her very much.

The boat chugged on monotonously for nearly an hour, passing islands crowned with dilapidated-looking buildings. There was no sign of the Venice people raved about, the Venice

David had hoped to show her. But in the distance, gradually growing larger and clearer, was an immense white object which she suddenly recognised as the *Hellene*, decked overall with fairy lights in honour of the new arrivals.

She was a welcome sight, dear and familiar. Coming back to her was like coming home. Reaching the quay at last, Jill looked up at the huge side of the ship, like a great block of flats. Perhaps it was foolish to hope that David might be watching out for her, but she hoped it nevertheless.

There was no sign of him but she found a note pushed under her door.

'If you're still interested in going ashore, I think we could make it after all. They've been having a spot of bother with one of the turbines—nothing serious, but sailing time is put off for three hours. I'll stay in my cabin till I hear from you, so give me a ring as soon as you get back. David.'

Jill leapt to the phone and asked to be connected. In a few seconds she heard his voice.

'I've got your note,' she told him breathlessly, 'and I'd love to go into Venice. How long can you give me to get ready?'

'Ten minutes. How did it go? The trip, I mean?'

'No problems at all. But I'm glad I went, all the

same, especially now I've got my outing after all. See you!'

Leaving her clothes in a heap on the floor, she had a quick shower and dressed hastily in a jade green skirt and long-sleeved black blouse with a small stand-up collar. She made up her eyes carefully and added a touch of lipstick. Snatching her fleecy shawl from the cupboard, she was ready.

David was looking very smart himself in well-cut trousers, a cream silk shirt and light jacket. His hair shone and a faint scent of after-shave hung about him.

Leaving the ship again meant battling against a stream of arriving passengers but they eventually reached the quay and boarded a *vaporetto*.

'We'll keep the gondola for later on,' David said, 'if there's time.'

Jill nodded happily. She was staring about her as the boat carried them smoothly through the water towards St Mark's Square. It was nearly dark now and the shabbiness of the buildings was hidden from her enchanted eyes. She saw only the beautiful romantic Venice of which she had dreamed.

They dined at a small restaurant tucked away in an alleyway leading out of the square. To reach it they had walked past the Doge's Palace and the great cathedral of St Mark's, but there was water on the other side, rippling gently against the ancient crumbling wall.

David was an ideal escort. He admired the outfit she had chosen to wear, his eyes telling her how much she attracted him. He kept the conversation going with ease and sophistication. It was almost, Jill thought in an unguarded moment, as if he were playing a role.

As soon as the thought was born she banished it from her mind in disgust. Just because he was making a good job of taking a girl out for the evening, there was no need for her to accuse him of acting. Of course he was sincere!

'Happy?' he asked, looking at her across his wine glass.

'So happy I'm almost frightened.'

'What on earth are you on about? You shouldn't be afraid of happiness, Jill. It's everyone's right.'

'Is it? An awful lot of people don't seem to achieve it.'

'That's true,' he agreed more seriously. 'I guess we've both seen plenty of unhappiness when we were working in London.'

'What made you become a ship's doctor?' Jill looked at him curiously. 'Did you want to travel, like me, and get paid for it?'

'Travel had nothing to do with it, though I've enjoyed seeing so many places for free.' He hesitated, staring down at his plate. 'I suppose you could say it was a combination of things. I had a very bad car crash and made a rotten job of getting over it. The surgeons who put me together again suggested that I should take it easy for six months. That meant opting out of the rat race and taking this post as ship's doctor.'

'But you seem so fit!' Jill exclaimed in astonishment.

'I am now, thank goodness. And my exile from the London hospital scene will be up in July. I shall be streaking back as fast as I can, that's for sure. I only hope I haven't slipped too far down the ladder during my absence.'

'Even if you have, I expect you'll soon climb up again,' she said warmly.

He smiled at her. 'Just what I wanted to hear you say, love, and I hope you're right. I've set my sights on being a consultant before I'm thirty. That gives me another two years.'

Jill sat quietly for a moment, thinking about what he had just told her. Somewhere, beyond the window, a man was singing something from one of the famous operas. The sound drifted across the water, as liquid as the canal itself.

Glancing at the tanned face opposite, the firm mouth and chin, she had no doubts at all that he would succeed in his ambition if he gave his mind to it. And that was obviously what he intended to do. An old saying came unbidden into her mind

'He travels fastest who travels alone,' and just for a moment she was horribly, humiliatingly on the verge of tears.

She winked them away with a fierce determination and gave her attention to what David was saying.

'I signed on last Christmas and we spent the first three months cruising in the Bahamas. I was getting pretty bored when the ship was switched to the Med. The cruise which is just starting is my fourth in this part of the world.'

With lowered lashes she tried to remember who had recently mentioned the Bahamas in her hearing. Oh yes, of course, it was the girl on the plane.

'I expect you'll soon get fed up with the Med too,' she said a little despondently.

'Not so much now you've come, Jill.' He leaned forward and touched her hand lightly. 'We must try and fix it so we can go ashore together as much as possible on this cruise. The first place the ship calls at is new to me too. Did you know we were going to Dubrovnik in Yugoslavia? We must explore it together.'

When they left the restaurant there was still enough time to hire a gondola and drift slowly down the canal, past elegant painted facades and the spires and cupolas of churches. David's arm was about her and her head rested on his shoulder, and the gondolier observed them with an indulgent smile between the slow rhythmic movements of his pole.

He preferred lovers as passengers. They rarely objected to his charges.

CHAPTER NINE

'WOULDN'T it be marvellous,' Jill murmured, 'if this could go on for ever?'

David laughed and lightly kissed the top of her head. 'For ever is a long time. We'd both be cold and sleepy and desperately bored—'

'*Must* you be so prosaic? You know I didn't mean it literally.'

'Of course you didn't, love. I was only teasing.'

They did not speak again until the gondola trip was over. By contrast, the *vaporetto* which took them back to the ship was noisy and crowded, an unavoidable reminder that the magic evening was over.

When they reached the *Hellene*'s great bulk, David halted and drew Jill into the shadow of the customs shed.

'Let's say goodnight here.'

It was an unromantic spot and she would have preferred somewhere on board, perhaps high on the top deck with only the stars and the fairy lights for company. But she went into his arms willingly enough and made no protest when his mouth fastened fiercely and demandingly on her own.

For a while they stood closely entwined, still half bewitched by the spell Venice had cast upon them, reluctant to return to their ordinary everyday life on board.

'I'm very grateful to that faulty turbine,' David said, when he at last loosened his grip. 'It's given me an evening to remember.'

'Me too,' Jill whispered.

'Did Venice come up to your expectations?'

'You know it did.'

'You're lucky to have seen it for the first time at night. It's got plenty of features that are better hidden by darkness, and sometimes it smells. Perhaps you didn't know that.'

Jill broke away from him and almost stamped her foot. 'Are you deliberately trying to ruin everything by talking like that?'

'Of course not. I was only bringing you back to earth as gently as I could. It seemed to me you were a bit moonstruck.'

'If that's what you call being gentle—talking about *smells*—'

He laughed and put his finger under her chin, tilting her face upwards. 'I enjoy making you angry, Jill. Your eyes flash and your cheeks turn pink with rage, and you look even more attractive than you do normally.'

His eyes were looking deep into hers and she

hastily lowered her lashes in case he should see—beneath the superficial anger—the depth of her love for him.

She said in a small determined voice, 'I shall always think of Venice as I saw it tonight and, for your information, I like being moonstruck. So please don't bother any more to try and spoil things.'

'I'm sorry, Jill.' David sounded genuinely repentant. 'I'm afraid I was teasing you again and I certainly didn't want to leave you with an unpleasant memory of the evening. It was wonderful for me too—you must know that.'

He kissed her again though with more restraint and then they went on board, walking hand-in-hand. They did not linger in the corridor leading to their cabins and Jill was glad. She was suddenly so tired that she longed only for the day to end.

She slept soundly and awoke refreshed and with a feeling of happiness. The ship was at sea and she dressed quickly and ran lightly right up to the top deck, thinking with amusement of that morning not so very long ago when she had slipped and sprained her ankle.

She had learnt a lot since then and she felt pleasantly detached as she watched the new passengers finding their way about the ship. They looked very much like the last lot, and it wasn't until she was leaving the dining room after breakfast that she saw someone who was different, and yet familiar. The girl on the plane.

She was wearing brief white shorts this morning and a sleeveless scarlet top. Her fair hair hung gleaming and silky beneath a wisp of head scarf and the brilliance of her eyes was enhanced by skilfully darkened lashes. They passed very close to each other and Jill was on the verge of saying, 'Hullo' when she realised that there was no sign of recognition on the other's face.

There was still a little time to spare before surgery and she went onto the promenade deck. David was standing near the board where Toni's photographs were usually displayed. It was empty now but there was a list of names hanging next to it and he was studying it with fixed attention.

'What are you looking at?' Jill went close to him and was surprised when he started violently. 'Did I make you jump? I'm sorry.'

'I was miles away,' he said carelessly.

'You certainly looked absorbed.' She stood on tiptoe and discovered he had been reading the passenger list. 'Anybody interesting on board?'

'Interesting? That's a bit much to hope for. I always look at the list, though, just in case there's someone I know.'

'And is there?'

There was no reply. David seemed to have retreated into some strange remote place where Jill could not follow him.

Puzzled, she went on her way. And it was not until she passed through the lounge on her way to the surgery that Danielle cleared up the mystery for her.

The dancers had assembled for their morning practice but their trainer had not yet arrived and Danielle left them to accost Jill.

'Guess what!' she said breathlessly.

'How can I guess when I haven't a clue what's in your mind?' Jill asked, not unreasonably.

'I can tell you in three words. Sonia is back! And as a passenger too. Isn't it extraordinary?'

'Sonia?'

'Your predecessor—the nurse who was with us when we were cruising in the Bahamas. Don't you remember me telling you about her?'

'Oh yes—of course I do.' Jill hoped her face was as blank as she was trying to make her voice sound. She hadn't really needed to repeat the name in that half-witted manner. She could re-call every single word Danielle had told her about the previous nurse.

'What on earth do you suppose she's doing on board as a passenger?' she added hurriedly, since some comment was obviously expected of her.

'Goodness knows, though I suppose she's entitled to turn up again in a new role. Seems kinda funny, though,' she added thoughtfully.

Jill said nothing and the dancer changed the subject.

'By the way, we're all going to the disco tonight. It's the Captain's welcome party for the passengers and the dancers have a night off. Will you come?'

Jill accepted with alacrity. So far she had never got to the disco. First her ankle had made it impossible, and then Malcolm—who had suggested they should go together—had caught his cold and retreated into self-pity, and she hadn't much cared to go alone.

The dancing mistress in charge of the four girls had arrived and Danielle said goodbye. Jill walked on slowly, wishing rather desperately that two and two didn't so obviously make four.

Every instinct she possessed was telling her that Sonia and the glamorous blonde were one and the same. No wonder David had appeared to be in a state of shock.

As clearly as though she were back on the plane she could hear that quick, high voice echoing through her head. *'I'm going to meet my fiancé—my fiancé—my fiancé—'*

Jill drew a long quivering breath and fought for self-possession. By the time she reached the surgery she had achieved at least an appearance of calm.

The door stood wide open and David was sitting at the desk, turning the pages of The Lancet. He greeted her mechanically, as though they had not already met that morning, and returned to his magazine. Unable to endure the terrible heavy silence, Jill went into the little hospital and busied herself with jobs that didn't need doing. As time passed she began to long for patients to arrive—lots of them with all sorts of complaints—so that she wouldn't have to be alone with David any longer.

There was so much she wanted to say, so many questions she needed to ask. But she wasn't supposed to know anything about Sonia; she must simply wait and see what happened.

What happened was that Sonia herself appeared.

It was nearly time to close the door. They had had only two patients, one requiring indigestion tablets and the other sleeping pills. Apart from that nothing had occurred to break open the vacuum in which they seemed to be encased.

And then there was a light step outside in the corridor and the tall slender blonde stood poised in the doorway. For a moment she remained there, as though posing for a photograph, and then she came in with all the confidence of familiarity. Her eyes were on David and Jill was totally ignored.

'Darling—it seems absolutely *years*! How are you? Still dishing out pills and bandaging cut fingers?'

'Of course.' His tone was carefully neutral but, glancing at him quickly, Jill noted that he had gone rather white round the mouth. 'It would be more to the point if I asked how *you* are, Sonia. I was very surprised to see your name on the passenger list.'

She sat down on the edge of the desk, swinging one long lightly-tanned leg. 'I'm quite well now, you know, and there was never much the matter with me anyway—nothing that couldn't be cured by a month's rest. Anyway, I thought I'd like to see—er—the dear old ship again.' She tilted her head back, gazing at him from beneath her lashes. 'Any objections?'

'None whatever,' David said bleakly. 'You've got as much right here as anyone else. But I can't help remembering that you declared very fervently that you'd had enough of the *Hellene* and everyone on board.'

'A girl can change her mind.'

Busying herself in the background with tidying up, Jill dropped a pair of scissors. The small sound seemed startlingly loud and, as they both turned to look at her, she muttered an apology.

'You two girls should get to know each other,' David said with a heartiness so false Jill could hardly bear it.

'We met yesterday on the plane,' she told him in a brittle voice.

'Did we?' Sonia's surprise sounded genuine. 'You probably look quite different in uniform.'

'We sat next to each other, actually.'

'I don't remember much about the flight.'

Jill made a move towards the door. 'You two will want to talk about old times. I'm going up on deck to lie in the sun.'

'Such a shame to have to wear that awful dress instead of a bikini or shorts,' Sonia said. She waved her hand nonchalantly. 'See you some time.'

Sick at heart, Jill turned away. She left the door open and before she could flee out of earshot a light clear voice came floating after her, as though in pursuit.

'David, darling—I just had to come back. I missed you so terribly—'

She didn't understand what any of it meant; all she knew was that David was clearly shaken to the depths of his being by the unexpected reappearance of his one-time nurse. Whatever his feelings towards her might be, one thing was for sure. He was certainly not indifferent.

In a trance of misery Jill climbed to the top deck. There was a kind of look-out at the forward end, popular with the passengers when approaching a port, but this morning there was no one there at all. She leaned her elbows on the wooden parapet and gazed over the shining blue water. The scene was much the same as on her first morning, when she had been so enraptured by it and then, later on, had fallen so ignominiously.

She hadn't liked David at all then and it had been a blow to discover he was her boss. And then, in such a short time, dislike had turned to liking and then to love.

And now?

She thought she knew the answer to that question. About her own feelings there could be no doubt, but for David their brief romance—if you could call it that—had been nothing more than a means of passing the time. As soon as Sonia came back his interest in Jill had vanished.

With a muffled sob she put both hands over her face, shutting out the brilliant scene which had given her so much pleasure. Its loveliness had no healing power; it merely seemed to intensify the pain.

She stood there for a very long time, glad of the solitude, and then she heard voices behind her and a family party appeared, the children delighted at being so high up.

Jill left her outpost, smiled automatically at the excited boy and girl, and made her way down again. On the boat deck she found Toni with his camera.

He had rapidly recovered from his misadventure at Crete, though the stitches in his head had not yet been taken out. He greeted Jill cheerfully and, after a quick glance at her face, asked her what was the matter.

'Nothing's the matter,' she assured him.

'Is not true.'

'Of course it's true. Why should anything be wrong? It's a super day and we seem to have a nice crowd of passengers on board. So far none of them has come up with any problems.'

'Except one, I think,' Toni observed.

'What do you mean?' Jill looked at him curiously. 'We haven't had any difficult patients—hardly any at all, in fact. Perhaps you mean the girl who is expecting a baby soon? She seems to be okay, thank goodness.'

'I did not mean a patient. You should know by now, I think, that Sonia is here. That one, she is so beautiful I take many, many photographs of her, but I not like her. Not like her at all.'

'It's very strange that she should turn up again,' Jill said, carefully schooling her voice, 'but I don't see why you think she is likely to cause problems. She looks healthy enough.'

'Is healthy in body—yes.'

'You're talking in riddles.'

'What are these—riddles?'

By the time Jill had explained her meaning the subject of Sonia had been dropped, to her great relief. She had better do something about her own fixation, she told herself firmly, and it was with this in mind that she went into the lounge and joined the Greek dancing class which was held there sometimes.

After that she descended into the depths of the ship and swam up and down the pool until she was worn out. She would much rather have used the one on the open deck but that was for passengers only during normal hours.

As she towelled herself she was unhappily aware that she had managed to fill up only half the day.

The most important thing was not to go anywhere where she might meet David or Sonia. She spent the afternoon reading in her cabin, which was fresh and cool owing to the air conditioning, had a very early dinner and then prepared for the disco.

If she hadn't been basically unhappy she would have enjoyed it. Toni and Spiro were there, and a lot of the people she had become acquainted with during the last cruise. The half darkness and flashing lights were very little different from the discos she had been to during her hospital days. Mesmerised by the beat, Jill flung herself energetically into at least giving a good impression of a girl without a care in the world.

'Is hot,' Toni gasped after some time had passed.

'I should think that's the understatement of the year.'

'Please?'

'I only meant that I agreed with you,' Jill explained.

Toni raised his thick dark brows, shrugged and glanced at the open door. 'Fresh air would be nice—yes?'

She didn't really want to go up on deck with him. His amorous advances would be harmless enough but definitely unwelcome. As she hesitated, he slipped his arm in hers, taking her willingness for granted.

Jill sighed and surrendered. She liked Toni and was even quite fond of him, so what did it matter?

In a quiet corner of the boat deck she stood stiffly when he put his arms round her, neither objecting nor encouraging. But when he kissed her it was impossible to hide from him her total inability to respond.

Toni lifted his head and looked at her reproachfully. 'Is like kissing a statue in a museum. But you a warm living girl, Jill, not statue. Why you like this?'

'I—I don't know. I'm sorry—' She broke off helplessly as tears welled up into her eyes and overflowed.

Toni produced a clean handkerchief smelling strongly of scent and mopped her face. 'I said earlier you unhappy,' he observed. 'You tell me?'

She shook her head, immensely touched by his kindness but quite determined that her secret must remain inviolate. 'I'm all right, Toni dear. Everyone gets depressed sometimes and there isn't always a reason for it.'

'I think you have reason.'

She left that unanswered and leaned her head against his shoulder, conscious of his arm still about her and that it was vaguely comforting. They were standing in the shadow of one of the lifeboats, looking away from the sea and across the deck. And suddenly Jill became aware that they were not alone in that part of the deck.

Another couple had found a quiet corner on the opposite side, a tall dark man and a girl whose fair hair floated round her head in the breeze like a cloud. As Jill stared, unable to help herself, she lifted her arms and slipped them round the man's neck, drawing his head down to meet the lips she was so clearly offering.

Jill shuddered and turned her face against Toni's shoulder, closing her eyes tightly to shut out even the memory of that brief glimpse.

David and Sonia. There was no doubt about it at all.

The nurse had said on the plane that she was going to join her finacé and Jill believed that she now understood the whole situation. There had been some sort of a row about the time the ship left the Bahamas and Sonia had thrown up her job and stormed back to England.

David had missed her and had used Jill as a stop-gap. But everything had obviously been straightened out now and they were lovers again. He would have no further use for his present nurse, except in her professional capacity.

And a good thing too, Jill told herself fiercely, and with a complete lack of truth.

CHAPTER TEN

IT WAS easy for Jill to close her eyes to the sight of David and Sonia together, but quite impossible to control her thoughts. They went round and round in a whirlpool of confusion as she stood there with Toni's arms about her, and yet—in spite of the muddle—they seemed always to arrive at the same conclusion.

There was only one explanation for David's recent interest in herself. She had caught him on the rebound from Sonia, had perhaps soothed his masculine pride or even his bruised heart.

And now he had no need of her at all.

'Please,' she said abruptly, 'let's go below now. I'm horribly tired. It was a very long day yesterday and I think it's caught up with me.'

Although puzzled by her choice of words, Toni understood her meaning, gave his characteristic shrug and made no protest. They passed within a few yards of David and Sonia but Jill kept her head averted and did not know whether she had been seen or not.

Maybe they were too absorbed in each other and the pleasure of reunion to notice anyone else.

She found herself dreading going on duty again, and when she reached the surgery in the morning it was immediately apparent that yesterday's tension had not eased at all—if anything, it was slightly worse.

David gave her a very strange and searching look when she entered. For one crazy moment she thought she saw reproach in his eyes and she wondered if he had noticed her with Toni on the boat deck. Even so, he surely shouldn't have the nerve to look reproachful!

Just before closing time he suddenly broke the oppressive silence.

'The ship reaches Dubrovnik this afternoon.'

'Yes, I know.'

He paused and glanced at her almost as though he were asking for help with a difficult conversation, but Jill had none to offer.

'I hope you haven't forgotten that we agreed to explore the walled town together.'

How could she forget! Jill hastily lowered her lashes so he shouldn't see the pain in her eyes.

'I haven't exactly forgotten but I'm assuming that the arrangement is now off.'

'Why should it be off?' he asked coolly. 'When I undertake to do something I'm not in the habit of withdrawing from it without good reason. I have every intention of honouring the agreement I made with you.'

'That's big of you!' Jill flashed.

He raised his eyebrows but all he said was, 'And I'm expecting you to honour your part of the bargain.'

'It wasn't a *bargain*! It was an arrangement made between—' she floundered a little '—between friends. And I haven't the slightest intention of honouring it.'

Too angry now to avoid his gaze, Jill looked straight at him and noticed that he was pressing his lips together as though to restrain his temper.

'Why not?' he asked curtly.

'Do you really need to ask that question?'

'Yes, I do! I want to know your reason for backing out.'

She shrugged. 'If you can't guess what it is, then I'm certainly not going to tell you.'

'And *I*'m not going to accept your withdrawal!' David shouted, giving up all attempt to control himself. 'You'll come to Dubrovnik as arranged, Jill, and that's my last word on the subject.'

'It's not mine. I absolutely refuse to come. I—I've completely lost interest in Dubrovnik.'

'I don't care whether you're interested or not. I've got good reasons for wishing you to come but I don't propose to go into them now. And if you persist in refusing, then I shall be obliged to remind you that I'm entitled to *order* you to fall in with my wishes. You don't have any official free time, you know, for the simple reason that most of your time is more or less free, and I'm quite within my rights in insisting that you accompany me to Dubrovnik.'

Jill gasped and was momentarily speechless. As she struggled to put her fury into words, David seized his opportunity.

'That's settled then,' he said with a return to his former coolness. 'I'll meet you at the landing stage at two-thirty.' With a couple of long strides he reached the door. 'Will you lock up, please?'

Left alone, Jill thought angrily of the various replies she might have made if only she'd been quicker. It was too late to say them now but one weapon still remained to her—total disobedience of his 'orders'.

It never even entered her head that she might begin to weaken, yet somehow it happened. Right up to lunchtime she was still determined on rebellion and then she heard the various hostesses giving instructions in their different languages regarding the afternoon's expedition to Dubrovnik.

In spite of everything she still wanted to see the famous walled city quite badly. Why not give in and do as she'd been told after all? She wouldn't be committing herself to anything except ordinary sightseeing.

Consequently, despising herself a little, she changed out of uniform and put on a sleeveless blue cotton dress. Punctually at two-thirty she reached the landing stage attached to the ship and found a tender there, rapidly filling up with passengers. As she hesitated, seeing no sign of David, she heard his voice behind her.

'Hop in, Jill, and we'll follow you.'

We? Flinging a startled glance over her shoulder, she saw Sonia beside him, glamorous in a clinging jade green dress with a deep plunge neckline.

'Sonia asked if she could join us,' David went on smoothly. 'She's never been to Dubrovnik either.'

If it had been possible Jill would have turned and fled. But a sailor was holding out his hand to her and her body was poised for the jump into the boat. Mechanically she smiled at the man and thanked him, and then found a seat as far from the others as she could.

She saw nothing of the trip across the sparkling water, heard nothing of the comments of the passengers around her. Her heart was filled with a bitterness so intense that it blackened her whole outlook. Had David planned this deliberately to torment her?

It seemed more probable that it had happened exactly as he had said. He might even have welcomed the idea of a threesome in order to boost his masculine ego. Very well then—she would go along with it and show him that a threesome was popular with her too, that anything was better than being alone with him.

Consequently, when they eventually entered the city by a huge double gateway, she walked at Sonia's side and laid herself out to be friendly.

David had bought a guide and he began to read aloud from it. 'The church of St Saviour is one of the smallest in existence and should not be missed. It was erected in 1520 as a thanks offering after an earthquake—'

'I don't care when it was erected or why,' Sonia interrupted pettishly. 'And I don't like going round old churches. The smell of incense makes me feel sick.' She pointed to a flight of steps. 'Can't we go up there?'

'They lead to the path round the walls. I thought we might walk round later on after we've seen some of the sights.'

'Oh, all right,' she agreed ungraciously, and then brightened a little. 'Some of the shops look quite good. I'd like to see if there's anything worth buying.'

'What do you want to see, Jill?' David asked politely.

'Everything!' she said gaily, very carefully not looking at him.

Instead she stared up the long wide street, paved with some sort of creamy stone and lined with elegant buildings, cafés and shops, all roofed with rosy-red tiles. There was an outsize fountain on the right, making a cool splashing sound, and everywhere there were glimpses of the massive walls surrounding the whole city.

If only she could have come to this marvellous place alone with David . . . But it was no good letting herself think of what might have been.

'I'll come and look at the shops with you if you like,' she said to Sonia. Turning to David, she added, 'Why don't you go and look round the church, and then meet us at the top of the street?'

'Okay. I'll give you girls twenty minutes.'

The shops really were good, though the things they sold were very expensive. Window-gazing, and occasionally going inside, Jill and Sonia made their way slowly up the street. Jill bought an embroidered belt and Sonia some bangles, and their purchases drew them together for a little while.

'It's a super idea, having shopping precincts everywhere,' Sonia said as they approached the point where the street broadened into a square. 'A whole city with no traffic at all—it's extraordinary.'

'Dubrovnik is very small. It wouldn't work with a larger place.' Jill turned and looked back to see if she could see David's tall figure among the strolling crowds.

He emerged from behind a column with a knight in armour at the top, and joined them with a few strides.

'You're not to tell us who that guy is.' Sonia directed a brief glance upwards. 'I just don't care.'

'Maybe Jill would like to know?' he said quietly.

'I don't care either.' She flashed a smile at him and hoped he wouldn't notice its falseness. 'How about making a tour of the walls now?' she suggested. 'We might be able to see some of the other sights from there.'

'It'll be cooler too,' Sonia put in, fanning herself.

'I should think about the coolest place in all Dubrovnik is the Cathedral.' David looked round, trying to locate it. 'But it would certainly smell of incense. Perhaps we'd better do as Jill said.'

They walked down a narrow alley and found a way up. As they reached the top of the steps Jill gave a spontaneous exclamation of pleasure. At that point the immense fortifications upon which they were standing went down straight into the sea. The pearly whiteness of the walls was dazzling against the deep blue of the water below.

'There's a very good view of the city, just like we thought there'd be.' David turned his back on the sea and looked across the vista of cupolas, towers and chimney pots.

'You'll turn into a walking guide book if you don't watch it,' Sonia said crossly.

He ignored her and began studying the pages. Jill stood beside him, gazing entranced at the mediaeval splendours of Dubrovnik, backed by an unknown mountain which appeared to rise almost from the base of the walls.

'I've always dreamt of coming here, ever since I first heard of the place,' she said dreamily.

Just for a moment it seemed as though they were exploring the city together, as they had planned a few days ago. Sonia, for once, was silent, and they stood close together, pointing out various buildings and temporarily forgetful of the third member of the party.

They were both startled when she called out suddenly from behind them.

'There's an even better view up here!'

Sonia was standing on top of the wall itself, a vivid figure in her bright green dress. Her arms were outstretched and every line of her body showed to perfection against the sky.

David took a quick step forward. 'For God's sake, be careful!'

'I'm okay.' She laughed and tossed her hair back. She looked like the figurehead of some graceful sailing ship. 'I've never been afraid of heights.'

She was showing off, Jill decided. She hadn't liked being temporarily left out of things and this was her way of reclaiming David's attention.

She glanced at him and thought how desperately worried he looked—which was only to be expected seeing that the girl he presumably loved was fooling about inches from a frightening drop into the rocky sea.

'If you must stand up there,' he was saying with rigid self-control, 'do come farther from the edge.'

'But I like looking down into the water.' Sonia deliberately moved a little nearer, leaning forward slightly. 'This would be a super place to commit suicide, wouldn't it? I wonder how many people have thrown themselves down from here, over the centuries.'

'Hundreds, I should think,' Jill said calmly.

Inwardly she was a little alarmed. She didn't like heights herself and would never have thought of climbing up there. Besides, there had been something strange about Sonia's laugh, a sort of wildness and an odd excitement perhaps caused by the proximity of danger.

'If you're so keen on views, Jill, why don't you come up and join me?' she taunted. 'You can see a lot more from here, like I said.'

'I've got more sense, thanks. You might take it into your head to push me over.'

'That's an idea! Maybe you'd better stay where you are in case I get tempted.'

David made an explosive sound of anger. 'Are you two girls completely crazy?'

'*I*'m not,' Jill said disdainfully. She turned her

back and began to walk on. 'There's not much point in an exhibition without an audience so why don't you come away too, David? She'll soon come down when there's no one to look at her.'

But apparently he couldn't bring himself to do that and Jill had covered some distance before they caught her up. Sonia was silent and sulky and she wondered what he had said to her, whether he had pleaded or scolded.

It was hard to imagine him pleading, but whatever method he had adopted it was only too clear that the incident had upset him badly.

She didn't enjoy their tour of the walls, magnificent as the views were. It was a relief when David suggested returning to the ship.

Sonia maintained her sulky silence until they were back on board. As Jill left them she couldn't help overhearing what sounded like the beginning of an indignant outburst.

'Why on earth did you insist on bringing *her* along, David? It was a perfectly horrible afternoon and—'

Hastily removing herself out of earshot, she couldn't help agreeing with the comment. Surely David couldn't have enjoyed it either? Or had it amused him to see the two girls alternately sparring and pseudo-friendly?

She wouldn't put it past him!

In the morning, when they were at sea again,

Toni came to the surgery to have his stitches out. He arrived just as they were about to lock up.

'You're late,' David said curtly, frowning down at the shorter man.

'You have date?' Toni suggested. 'Then I not keep you. Is easy to take stitches out—yes? Jill can do it.'

'I expect you'd rather have her anyway.' David produced a frosty smile. 'So I'll leave you together.'

He left at once and Jill went over to the sink and began to scrub her hands. Toni sat down and stared thoughtfully at her backview.

'I think the doctor goes to join Sonia. She has two chairs all ready in a quiet corner.'

Jill was using the brush so vigorously that her skin glowed pink in the soapy water. She worked hard for a moment and then produced a would-be casual comment.

'Why shouldn't he join Sonia? She told me she was on holiday with her fiancé, and she couldn't have meant anyone else.'

Toni shrugged. 'I know nothing except that they always together when she was the nurse. Together in bed too, I expect. Sonia very beautiful girl and any man want to go to bed with her.'

'Yes, but that isn't the same as wanting to *marry* her.' Keeping her back still turned, she began to dry her hands on a clean towel.

Toni ignored the comment. He was staring at her in some apprehension. 'You not hurt me, Jill?'

'I'll be very careful.' She gave him an encouraging smile and started work.

Toni screwed up his eyes and assumed an expression of endurance and Jill went mechanically along the line of sutures, snipping each stitch and withdrawing it gently. When he opened his eyes again she had moved away.

'Is finished?' he asked in surprise.

'Yes, and I don't believe you felt anything at all. You'll be able to comb your hair over the scar more easily now. But please don't get into any more brawls when you go ashore. You might not come off so lightly next time.'

He promised solemnly to be careful, and Jill smiled and reminded him he would have an opportunity to keep his promise when the ship reached Corfu.

She ought to have been looking forward to going ashore herself, since she had missed visiting the island owing to her sprained ankle the last time the ship was there. She was quite determined that she *would* see Corfu, but looking forward to enjoying the trip was another matter altogether. It was with a heavy heart concealed beneath a bright and brittle manner that she approached David for the necessary permission.

'It would be a pity to miss it again,' he said with

formal politeness, 'but please check with me before you actually leave the ship.'

'Yes, of course,' she agreed with a stiffness which matched his.

'I shall be leaving the ship for a short time myself but it should be okay for us both to be away for a while.'

'We've done it before,' Jill said, and was aghast to hear the bitterness in her voice.

'Occasionally.' He had been staring across the top of her head but now he dropped his gaze to her face. 'You're not going alone, I hope?'

'Yes, I am!' Anger flared suddenly in her eyes. 'And I prefer it that way, so if you were going to suggest another threesome, you can think again. Our visit to Dubrovnik was the most boring and uncomfortable I've ever experienced. Sonia may be the most beautiful girl on board but as a sightseeing companion she's nothing but a disaster. No doubt you find her totally satisfying but I'm afraid I don't.'

She stopped abruptly, dismayed by the rage she saw in his face.

'You imagine I'm the sort of man who gets swept off his feet by a pretty face?'

'Well—yes, that's exactly what I do think, though, of course, it's probable that Sonia has got other attractions I wouldn't know about.'

'How dare you!' David seized her by the shoulders and shook her violently. 'You know nothing at all about the relationship between Sonia and me.'

'It's not hard to guess.'

'And very easy to guess wrong.'

If it had been possible Jill would have shrugged her shoulders in disbelief but his fingers were pressing deeply into her flesh and she was held a prisoner. Consequently she took refuge in silence, tilting her chin defiantly and glaring back at him.

His eyes were like cold hard steel and it was difficult to believe that he had ever looked at her with what she had hoped might be love. But suddenly his mood changed. He bent his head and she felt the sudden impact of his mouth on hers, forcing her lips back against her teeth until she would have cried out in pain had she been able to.

It was a violent kiss, with nothing of tenderness in it, and she broke away from him with a strangled sound very like a sob, fleeing away down the corridor towards the sanctuary of her cabin.

CHAPTER ELEVEN

ONCE more Jill stood staring across half a mile of sunlit water at the green loveliness of Corfu. It looked just as she remembered, with the grim backcloth of mountains throwing into relief the pastel-painted houses of the little town. It wasn't the island's fault that nothing but bleak determination was sending her ashore.

Later on, when she actually set foot in Corfu Town, she found it fully lived up to her original expectations. There were long rows of Judas trees decked with bright pink flowers and beds of cinerarias in every conceivable colour. There was an ancient church and fascinating shops behind a cream-washed colonnade. And, as an added bonus, some sort of religious procession was wending its way across the square.

As Jill stood staring a middle-aged man from the ship accosted her.

'All alone, Nurse? If you're looking for your friends—the doctor and the other girl—they went thataway.' And he pointed down a side street.

'Thanks.' Jill smiled and hoped he wouldn't

notice when she hurried off in a different direction.

It would have been funny if it hadn't been so utterly horrible. And when she actually saw David and Sonia coming towards her and was obliged to dive into a shop, Jill decided that the situation was bad enough without developing elements of farce. She would return to the *Hellene* and postpone a proper exploration until they called there again.

It was one of the most important decisions she had ever made in her whole life but nothing warned her of that at the time. All she felt as she walked slowly across the sunlit square was a deep sense of depression.

She was close to the turning which would take her towards the quay when she saw a flash of brilliant pink on her right. Sonia—alone and wearing a flamboyant sundress—was going into a gift shop on the corner.

Jill had barely registered the fact when she was again accosted by a passenger.

'Nurse!' A thin young man with an anxious face and a thatch of straw-coloured hair was running towards her and waving to attract her attention. 'Thank God I happened to see you!' He reached her side, panting.

'What's the matter?' she asked in surprise.

'It's my wife. She's got this terrible pain— came almost out of the blue—and we're afraid it might mean she's started in labour though the baby's not due for another month. Do please come and see her.'

'Where is she?'

'Sitting on that seat over there.' He seized Jill by the arm, as though afraid she might escape, and began to tow her towards a seat under one of the Judas trees.

As they approached Jill recognised the young woman she had seen first when the ship's new passengers were arriving. Since then she had noticed her once or twice lounging in a deck chair but she had not been to the surgery at all.

'I had a stroke of luck, Kathy,' the man said. 'Just happened to see the nurse walking along all alone.' He turned to Jill again. 'I was actually looking for a taxi, so we could get back to the ship as quickly as possible.'

Jill was studying this unexpected patient with a professional eye and, privately, she agreed with the husband that finding a taxi was of some urgency. Outwardly, though, she preserved an appearance of coolness and calm.

'Your baby won't arrive within the next five minutes, Kathy. I'm quite sure there's plenty of time to get you back and comfortably settled. But I don't think you should try to walk any farther than necessary. Your husband can stay with you and I'll fetch a taxi.'

There was something else she must do first.

Walking as quickly as she could without appearing to hurry too much, Jill returned to the spot where she had glimpsed Sonia. Almost certainly she would still be inside the shop.

In spite of the crowd of people it was easy to locate her because of the dress. She was staring at some jewellery, picking up one necklace after another and then flinging it down impatiently.

Jill wasted no time.

'Sonia—' She appeared suddenly at her side, making the other girl jump violently. 'Where's David?'

The skilfully darkened eyebrows were drawn into a frown. 'What's that got to do with you?'

'I've got a patient for him—a maternity case. I'm going to escort her back to the ship but I think he should see her as soon as possible. It won't be long before the baby arrives.'

Sonia's expression did not change. 'Can't you manage on your own?'

'I'm not a qualified midwife though I did Part I. You've got to tell me where David is—it could be terribly important.'

'He's around somewhere.' Sonia shrugged and Jill resisted a strong desire to shake her. 'I'll tell him if you like but I'm sure it's not necessary. He'd probably be back on board in plenty of time in any case.'

'You *promise* you'll tell him?'

'I just said so, didn't I?'

Jill hesitated, not at all convinced that Sonia would keep her promise a moment sooner than it suited her to do so.

'Please tell him quickly,' she begged. 'I daren't stay here any longer arguing with you but it really is terribly important.'

'Okay, okay,' Sonia said impatiently, swinging her hair like a curtain between her face and Jill's searching eyes. 'Hadn't you better get back to your patient?'

The unsatisfactory conversation was clearly finished. Hoping for the best, Jill hurried outside again and looked about for a taxi. She was fortunate in finding one almost at once and the driver seemed to understand English. Within seconds he had stopped near the seat where Kathy sat with her husband.

It was an anxious trip back to the *Hellene*. They reached the quay in a very short time, but the men in charge of the tender did not want to leave until they had more passengers. None of them spoke English well and Jill felt that her passionate plea was being disregarded.

Fortunately another tender arrived just then, bringing members of the crew and among them Jill spotted Toni.

'Toni!' She flung herself towards him and clutched his arm. 'Please come and help—these men are so thick! You'd think they would guess what's happened just by looking at Kathy.'

Rapidly she explained her problem.

'Is my pleasure,' Toni said gallantly when he had done what she asked.

She thanked him profusely and went to help Kathy into the boat. With cries of alarm and some show of sympathy, the crew started the engine and set out across the shining water.

Watching the *Hellene* growing steadily larger, Jill wished with all her heart that David was with them in the tender. She couldn't even be sure that he would join them quite soon, since he might have the same difficulty in persuading the Greeks to convey him to the ship. Assuming that Sonia had bothered to tell him.

As the tender bumped gently against the landing stage she stood up and shaded her eyes, gazing back towards Corfu. She could see no sign of activity on the quay at all. The second tender was motionless, its crew probably dozing in the hot sun.

'Oh God—' Kathy's face was ashen and beads of sweat glistened on her forehead. 'I never knew it would be like this—not so soon.'

'You'll feel better when I've got you settled in the hospital.' Jill put her arm round her patient and helped her to walk into the ship.

'Hospital?' The father-to-be turned an astonished face towards them.

'Oh yes—we're prepared for anything on the *Hellene*.'

As they went up in the lift, she found herself hoping it was true. She knew there was a sterile maternity pack in one of the cupboards, but were they prepared for what might be a difficult birth? They didn't have blood, for instance, and their anaesthetic equipment was only what was ordinarily used for simple operations.

'You'll stay with me, Gavin?' Kathy begged as they reached the door of the surgery. 'I don't want to be left here by myself.'

'Of course I'll stay, love,' he said fondly, though Jill sensed that he was dreading the ordeal even more than his wife. 'But you won't really be alone, you know. Nurse will be here and the doctor won't be long.'

He went off to fetch a nightdress and toilet articles. As Kathy writhed on the bed and moaned to herself, Jill timed the pains and was alarmed to find that the interval between them had shortened considerably.

As soon as Gavin returned she left husband and wife together and began to collect what would be needed. Remembering the sophisticated equipment available in hospital, she couldn't help feeling that the *Hellene*'s maternity supplies were pathetic. Not that you could really expect anything else—people weren't supposed to have babies on cruise ships.

When she had done everything possible, she excused herself for a moment and went to put her uniform on. Properly dressed, she felt a little more confident.

The pains were coming faster now and she insisted on Gavin dressing in a sterile gown and mask. Kathy stared at him during a brief moment of calm and even burst into a gasping sort of laugh.

'You do look funny!' She turned her head and stared round the little hospital. 'Isn't the doctor here yet? I can't have my baby until he comes.'

Jill resisted the temptation to say 'It doesn't look as though you'll have much option,' and stole a glance at her watch. Two hours since she had given Sonia the message. David should have arrived long ago—and once again she had to add the proviso '*if* he knows anything about the emergency.'

She felt more than ever sure that he did not.

Suddenly she had an idea. People would be returning to the ship by now and he would probably be among the first. If she could get a message broadcast he would hear it and come at once.

It took only a moment to call the purser's office from the phone in the surgery. Speaking softly, so as not to be overheard in the next room, Jill told the Greek at the other end what she wanted.

'Not to worry, Nurse,' he said cheerfully. 'Will do.'

Not to worry . . . Jill's lips twisted in a rueful smile as she re-adjusted her mask. As though she could help worrying!

And yet, during the next twenty minutes, she forgot all about it. There just wasn't time to give in to her own apprehension. Kathy kept her too busy.

'Don't bother to try and be brave,' Jill urged her patient. 'Yell as much as you like if it helps you. Nobody will hear you in here.'

Gavin was looking as though he might faint at any moment but he still clung to his wife's hand. In a very brief moment of detachment Jill wondered which was receiving most encouragement from the other.

So far everything had gone well, in spite of the speed of labour. But as Kathy made one last tremendous effort and her tiny son slipped into the world, one glance at his face told Jill that here was a problem indeed. He was a month too soon and his small strength had been exhausted by his precipitate arrival. He wasn't going to trouble himself to make an attempt to breathe.

Now, as never before, she needed help. And it seemed like a miracle when help came.

The door from the surgery opened and David strode in. He summed up the situation in one glance and came straight over to Jill.

'Give me the baby and you stay with the mother,' he ordered.

She wrapped the child in a clean towel and handed him over. As she checked Kathy's condition and dealt as best she could with her eager questions, her whole being seemed tuned in to what was happening behind her.

Suddenly there was a tiny feeble wail of protest which grew steadily stronger and ended in a roar.

'Please let me see him,' the mother begged. 'Why did you take him away before I'd had a chance to look properly?'

Fortunately she did not seem to expect any reply to her question, and when David brought the baby to her she cradled him in her arms and crooned over him.

'Is he going to be all right?' Jill asked in an undertone later on when David was peeling off his rubber gloves after making sure that all was well with Kathy.

'I think so. He's not very big, of course, but he doesn't need an incubator. Which is fortunate, since we don't have one,' he added grimly.

As Jill started on the task of tidying up he looked at his watch and then sent Gavin off to have his dinner.

'I'll get something sent in for you and the mother,' he said briskly, 'and then when I've had my own meal we can get down to it.'

'Down to what?'

'You know perfectly well,' he said coldly, and went out.

Jill stared at the closed door and then turned away with a weary shrug. What with one thing and another it had been quite an evening and she hadn't nearly finished yet.

She persuaded Kathy to eat a little food and then consumed her own hungrily. She felt better after that but still not at all in a mood to 'get down to it' with David.

When he came back he had Gavin with him and was telling him he was going to leave him in charge.

'Be sure to call for help at once if you have any problems,' he said. 'I'm not anticipating any but it's as well to be prepared. Either the nurse or I, or both, can be here within a few minutes.' He turned to Jill. 'Ready?'

Mentally she was far from ready but she no longer had any duties to detain her. And so she nodded without speaking and they left the surgery together.

'You could probably do with a drink,' David told her in a peremptory tone, 'and so we'll have our talk in the nearest bar.'

'I'm not allowed to go in the passengers' bars. The Staff Captain wouldn't like it.'

'The Staff Captain can lump it. You'll be coming as my guest.'

After the emotion-charged atmosphere of the

tiny hospital where the miracle of birth had taken place, it seemed strange to be back in the world of holidaymakers. The bar was hot and noisy, and full of well-dressed people. Jill, still in her uniform, was glad to hide herself in a corner while David fetched their drinks.

'Now—' He looked straight at her across a silver vase of pink carnations, his eyes very searching. 'I want to ask you a question, Jill. Why the hell didn't you send for me earlier? Don't you realise that you were putting the lives of both mother and child at risk?'

She stared back at him blankly, her tired mind floundering hopelessly. A schoolgirlish sense of honour made her reluctant to 'tell on' Sonia and yet she knew she ought. The matter was too serious to be disregarded.

'Are you a qualified midwife?' David persisted.

'No.'

'Then *why*?' He waited but she still said nothing and he went on inexorably. 'I came back to the ship quite early. I'd been on board for half an hour when the message came over the loudspeakers. So you could easily have got my help earlier if you hadn't decided you could manage on your own. What on earth possessed you, Jill?'

She said stiffly, 'I didn't decide I could manage on my own. I'm not such a fool.'

'Then perhaps you'll be kind enough to explain.'

'I—I met Gavin and Kathy when I was in Corfu Town and they said she'd started in labour, so I came back to the ship with them.' She came to a full stop.

'That's when I should have been told,' he asserted firmly.

'How could I tell you when I didn't know where you were?'

'We were never far from the square and it would have been worth while spending a few minutes looking for us. Sonia was wearing a dress which could be seen a mile off.'

'Yes, I know.' Jill took a hasty sip of her drink but it tasted of nothing. 'I saw her but she—she was alone then.'

'When did you see her?'

She hesitated and David pounced. 'She wasn't on her own for long. It must have been just before you left Corfu and that means—' He broke off, his eyes raking her face. 'Did you give her a message for me?' he asked quietly.

Immensely relieved that he had stumbled on the truth without having it put into words, Jill at once admitted it.

'She didn't seem to think there was any need for haste as this was a first baby. I suppose that was why she didn't tell you.'

'I doubt it.' His lips had tightened. 'Sonia's

reasons are rarely as straightforward as that.' He drained his glass and stood up, apparently not even noticing that Jill had barely tasted hers. 'Come on. Let's go and have it out with her.'

'There's no need for me to come.'

'Of course there is.' He was impatient, already on his way. 'Don't mess about, Jill. This is desperately important.'

Reluctantly, and with deep foreboding, Jill got up and followed him out of the bar.

CHAPTER TWELVE

SONIA was in the big lounge, apparently waiting
for the evening entertainment to begin. She was
talking with great animation and much restless
movement of her hands to a sophisticated-
looking couple in their thirties.

When David approached she looked up, not at
first noticing Jill hovering in the background.

'So there you are, darling—I wondered what
had happened to you. Come and sit down.' She
patted the chair beside her invitingly.

'No, thank you. I'm not in the mood for floor
shows tonight.' His voice was icy and Sonia's
eyes widened in bewilderment. 'I want to talk to
you, but not here. Somewhere out on deck
would be best.'

She jumped up at once and slipped her arm
through his, ignoring his stiffness. But when she
saw Jill her expression changed.

'I don't know what David wants to talk to me
about but it can't possibly be anything to do with
you.'

He interposed swiftly before Jill could answer.
'It has everything to do with Jill, and if you can't

172

guess what it is you're even more irresponsible than I thought.'

'You *are* in a horrible mood tonight.' Sonia rubbed her head against his shoulder like a cat. 'I'm sure if I had any sense I'd stay here but you know I can't resist you when you order me about.'

Feeling thoroughly nauseated Jill followed behind as they went out and up to the boat deck. She wanted no part in the scene which was obviously going to take place, and whatever the outcome of it might be she couldn't feel it was likely to bring any happiness to herself.

'Now—' David halted when they reached a point as far forward as possible. 'I want to know why you didn't give me that very important message this afternoon?'

Sonia's eyes were large and innocent as they gazed up at him. 'What message?' she asked blankly.

'You know damned well what message.' He dragged his arm from her clinging fingers. 'Come on, Sonia—I want the truth and none of your fairy tales.'

'But I honestly don't know what you're on about,' she protested.

'Then Jill had better remind you.' He turned to her, his face thunderous. 'Go on—give it to her straight.'

'It was the message about the baby,' she said

briefly. 'You were in the gift shop when I spoke
to you.'

'I don't remember.'

'Don't be ridiculous—you *must* remember!
I told you that one of the passengers had started
in labour and asked you to let David know at
once.'

In the faint light Sonia's lovely face looked
totally devoid of expression. Even the brilliant
luminous eyes were blank.

'The first I heard of it was when the message
came over the loudspeakers,' she said indif-
ferently.

'You're lying!' David accused her furiously.

Jill thought so too. No normal person could
have forgotten anything as quickly as that.

'It was just luck that David arrived in time to
save the baby's life,' she burst out, 'and he could
have been there at least an hour earlier.'

Sonia tossed her hair back as the breeze blew it
across her face. 'I expect you're exaggerating,'
she declared scornfully.

Suddenly David lost his temper. 'It would
hardly be possible to exaggerate the enormity of
what you've done,' he stormed, seizing her by
the shoulders and shaking her. 'I've put up with a
lot from you, Sonia, but one thing I'm not prepared to tolerate is your endangering the lives of
my patients. I've had enough—do you hear? I
shan't be able to avoid seeing you around while

the cruise lasts, but after it ends I hope our paths never cross again.'

Jill gasped in complete bewilderment. David surely couldn't really mean that? He must have said it because he was in such a temper and he would regret it later. She looked at Sonia to see what her reaction was and instantly felt a reluctant pity for her.

The girl seemed utterly stricken. Her face was white and she was clenching and unclenching her hands as she struggled for words. When at last she found her voice it was choked with sobs.

'Oh, David, David—how could you say a thing like that to me! I—I can't bear it when you're angry with me. There's nothing left in life if you don't love me—nothing!'

'For God's sake, Sonia—' His tone was a mixture of rage and embarrassment.

'You know I can't live without you,' she went on, her voice rising uncontrollably. 'Why did I come back to the ship, if it wasn't because of you?'

'It's not my fault you were such a fool,' David told her brutally.

For a few seconds she stared at him blankly and then, with a loud cry of anguish, she turned to flee.

'Sonia—' He took a step forward and tried to catch her arm but she was too quick for him.

'Let me go—you don't care what happens to me—' With the speed of frenzy she raced across the open space and reached the steps leading to the next deck.

'I should never have spoken to her like that. I might have known shock tactics wouldn't work.' Distraught, David glanced at Jill. 'Come on, we've got to catch her before she does something utterly crazy.'

His long legs carried him across the deck and almost out of sight. Jill panted to the top of the steps in time to see him come to an abrupt halt as he looked about for Sonia. There was no sign of her but Jill thought she heard a slight sound from a further flight of steps which led up to the highest part of the ship, the look-out from which passengers sometimes took photographs of their arrival at a new port.

'I think she went up there.' She pointed to the steps.

David set off again and she went rushing after him. At first she hadn't really believed Sonia meant to do anything more than frighten them, but somehow the danger seemed to grow more real the higher up they went.

Sonia had reached the look-out. They could see her outlined against the moonlit sky as she balanced on the edge of the parapet. It was just like it had been at Dubrovnik—only this time Jill felt convinced that she meant to throw herself over. Down, down and down to the hungry sea below.

She could hear herself screaming, 'Stop her—stop her!' as she flung herself in David's wake across the space which separated them from that frantic, tragic figure.

Just as he reached her, Sonia jumped.

It seemed a long, long time before they heard the tiny sound of a splash. As Jill stood rooted in despair David started running again.

'I'm going to the bridge. We must stop the ship and get a boat lowered.'

How on earth did one stop a ship the size of the *Hellene*? Jill's weary mind demanded as she galvanized her legs into further action. She made no attempt to follow David to the bridge but he must have convinced the duty officer of his integrity for very soon bells started ringing and the great vessel seemed to shudder all over.

There was a babbling sound from below as passengers streamed out of the lounge to see what was going on, some of them very much inclined to panic. Jill waited by the boats and it was there that David found her.

'You must come with me, Jill. I may need your help.'

'You're going in the lifeboat?'

'Of course,' he said impatiently.

'Do you think there's any chance of finding her?'

'You know damned well I can't answer that.'

One of the officers was calling to them and they climbed into the boat. It descended slowly and jerkily to the water, as though it was a long time since it had been farther than the level of the promenade deck for lifeboat drill. As the engine burst into life Jill shivered in her thin uniform dress and wrapped her arms about her.

They sat in silence as the boat swept round in an arc and turned back in the direction from which the *Hellene* had travelled. How did the sailors know how far to go before they began searching? Jill wondered.

'Could Sonia swim?' she asked suddenly.

'She could swim all right in the pool but—' David left the sentence unfinished.

She knew exactly what he meant. Swimming in the sea would be very different. Besides, Sonia might not even try.

The lifeboat was slowing down and a powerful light was switched on, turning the waves into liquid gold. David sat upright and stared out across the restless water as the boat slowly quartered an area with invisible boundaries.

Time passed unnoticed. Jill had no idea whether they had been searching for ten minutes or half an hour when suddenly one of the men shouted out something in Greek.

'There she is!' David had caught a glimpse of a waving arm almost at the same moment.

It seemed unbelievable that Sonia had found the strength to keep herself afloat for so long but somehow she had managed it. As she was hauled into the boat, a sodden dead weight, hair trailing like seaweed, she looked straight at David.

'I didn't want to die—it was all a mistake—' Her voice faded away and she lapsed into unconsciousness.

Blankets were produced from a locker and they wrapped Sonia in them, laying her down in the bottom of the boat with her head on Jill's lap.

'She's breathing quite normally,' David said. 'We'll leave her to come round in her own good time.'

After a while the starlight showed Jill that her patient's eyes were open.

'David?' Sonia whispered.

'He's here, right beside us.'

'Is he still angry?'

'No, of course not.' Jill smoothed back the wet hair. 'Don't worry about it any more. Just rest.'

They seemed to get back to the waiting *Hellene* very quickly, and they saw that her decks were lined with passengers. As the lifeboat was drawn up again a cheer broke out.

No doubt some of them had enjoyed it, Jill thought wryly. It would have been an added excitement. As for herself, she knew quite certainly that she never, never wanted to pass through such an experience again. It could so very easily have ended in tragedy.

'A hot shower and a sedative for you, Sonia,' David prescribed when they reached the corridor leading to her cabin. He glanced at Jill. 'I'll leave her to you.'

'What about Kathy and the baby?'

'I'm on my way to see them now and you'd better come along when you've finished here. It might be a good idea for you to sleep in the hospital tonight.'

Jill didn't care where she slept so long as it was somewhere. Wearily she helped to peel off saturated clothing, and as she did so a sense of unreality crept over her. Never in her wildest dreams could she have imagined this sort of situation occurring. Sonia was silent and docile, and seemed perfectly normal until she again reverted to her fantasy world.

'I didn't jump, you know. The ship sort of lurched and I lost my balance.' Her eyes opened very wide and fixed their gaze on Jill's face.

'Yes, of course. I quite understand how it happened, but don't worry about it any more—just go to sleep.'

As she waited for the sedative to take full effect, Jill's mind was busy. It was now quite clear to her that Sonia was mentally unstable and David, because he was a doctor, had tried to help her.

But had he another reason for taking so much interest in the case? Did he also love her? He had said harsh and cruel things just before her suicide attempt but they had been said in the heat of the moment when he was very angry. More than likely he now bitterly regretted them.

There was another question too. Why hadn't he taken Jill into his confidence about Sonia? To that, at least, she was determined to obtain an answer.

As soon as Sonia was deeply asleep, Jill left her cabin and went in search of David. She found him just leaving the hospital.

'Everything's okay in here,' he told her. 'Don't forget to make yourself up a bed. The baby's sure to need attention during the night.'

'I shan't forget.'

'Sonia all right?'

'If you can call it that.' Jill snatched at her opportunity. 'Why didn't you warn me she was mentally disturbed? I didn't suspect it for one moment. I just thought she was one of these over-excitable people—a bit inclined to be hysterical perhaps but nothing more.'

She was looking up at him searchingly, but instead of meeting her eyes he stared straight across the top of her head, as though reading his reply on the corridor wall.

'I hoped it wouldn't be necessary to tell any-one. After all I managed to keep it completely dark when we were in the Bahamas. And if I'd warned you, you'd have been for ever looking out for signs and symptoms. It would have been impossible for you to treat her naturally.'

'I didn't find that easy in any case! If I'd realised she was mentally ill I might have been a bit more sympathetic.' She hesitated and then plunged into another question. 'Did she have to be sent home before, when the ship was cruising in the Bahamas?'

'Yes.' His deadpan expression remained unchanged. 'Her father flew out and fetched her, and I'm arranging for him to do the same at Rhodes so her psychiatric treatment can be continued. He's a doctor so he knows how to cope.'

Suddenly he looked down at her and his face softened slightly. 'You look very tired, Jill. Better see about getting that bed made up.'

She nodded and went into the hospital, where she found Gavin and Kathy radiant, and the baby sleeping soundly. It was at least another hour before she finally got into bed and tried to sleep while at the same time remaining alert for any sign that she was needed.

Inevitably it was a broken night and in the morning Jill was still tired. Fortunately work soon cured that and she had plenty to do, with a maternity case and a would-be suicide on her hands. For forty-eight hours she was really busy, and then Kathy and her baby left the hospital and

Sonia was escorted to the airport at Rhodes to meet her father.

Jill had half expected she would get that job too but David went himself.

And then—quite suddenly it seemed—she had time to spare, far too much of it. Time for thinking and wondering, and coming at last to a great decision.

With a painful certainty she knew that she could neither contemplate continuing to work with David, nor working with anyone else when he left in July. Cruise nursing had gone sour on her and there was only one thing to be done. To give in her notice would be a wonderful solution.

That being so, it was strange that she felt no elation. Nothing except a deep sadness.

The Staff Captain's annoyance was tinged with resignation. 'Nurses, they come and they go. Almost one expects it. But one does not expect it with doctors.'

Jill stared at him, puzzling over what he had said and then shelved it as she went to convey her decision to David.

It took her some time to find him. He was not in any of the lounges nor on the promenade deck. Eventually she discovered him much higher up, leaning on the rail in a quiet corner of the top deck.

Wisps of cloud were drifting across the moon but the stars were bright and she could see him quite easily. Not giving herself time to be nervous Jill went straight up to him and called his name.

'David—can you spare a moment?'

He turned round quickly, obviously considerably startled. 'Of course,' he said in the formal polite tone which nowadays alternated with bad temper.

Jill came straight to the point. 'I wanted to tell you that I'm leaving the *Hellene*. I don't like cruise nursing as much as I thought I would.'

He stared at her in blank astonishment. 'You're leaving? But I thought you were so keen on travel—I thought you enjoyed shipboard life—' He broke off abruptly. 'What's the real reason, Jill?'

For one brief moment she was tempted to tell him. If she cried out in a crazy outburst of truth, 'I've been daft enough to fall in love with you,' what would his reaction be? Embarrassment? Disgust?

She put the temptation aside. 'I gave you my reason, but perhaps it could be enlarged a little. I think maybe I'm disillusioned—disappointed, if you like. I want to get back to hospital life and do a real job of nursing.'

'Nursing's been real enough for you recently.'

'For a few days.' Jill smiled wryly. 'And I didn't enjoy that much either.'

'I was afraid that business with Sonia had

upset you rather badly,' David said quietly. 'I think perhaps I was partly to blame for not being more frank with you.'

'You can say that again!' She hadn't meant to mention Sonia but suddenly words began to tumble out. 'I hated her at first but in the end I felt terribly sorry for her. She'd had a raw deal, hadn't she? You had an affair with her when she was your nurse—'

'Who the hell told you that?' he demanded, interrupting furiously.

'Everybody knew.'

'Then everybody was wrong. I never had an affair with Sonia, though I admit I found her attractive for a while.'

'I suppose you led her on and encouraged her to imagine you loved her, just like—' Jill broke off abruptly, horrified because she had almost added 'you did me.'

'I did nothing of the sort!' David shouted. He seized her by the shoulders and shook her. 'You've got to believe that, Jill.'

'Why have I?'

His reply was so astonishing that she gasped and was temporarily bereft of words.

'Because it's the truth, for one thing, but mostly because it's so important. It matters to me what you believe about me—it matters a hell of a lot. Didn't you know that?'

'No, I didn't,' she said forlornly, when she had

got her breath back. 'I didn't understand anything at all about you and me.'

'Good God, love!' His hands slipped off her shoulders and drew her close. 'I seem to have made a right mess of things and I was trying so hard too.'

Her heart was beating so violently that once more she found speech difficult, but somehow she managed to ask, 'What were you trying hard to do—or not do? I still don't understand.'

'Not to frighten you off, love, by going too fast and rushing you off your feet. I knew at the end of the first week that you were the girl I wanted to marry.'

'M-marry?'

'Yes—*marry*!' He was shouting again. 'Do I have to spell it out for you?'

Jill's thoughts were whirling and she never knew how she answered him, though it must have been all right because his arms tightened about her. The hard pressure of his mouth was sheer ecstasy and the feel of his long lean body pressed against her own sent her pulses racing and filled her with yearning for the moment when they could be truly one.

At last they drew a little apart and began to talk.

'I've got something to tell you,' David said. 'You aren't the only one who's leaving the ship soon. I had a letter the other day from my old boss. He wants me back urgently so that I can get slotted in again before his retirement in the autumn. He says I've got a good chance of landing a junior consultant's post then.'

'That's marvellous!' She was delighted for him. 'Will the shipping company release you before July?'

'I think so. Maybe we can leave together.'

They continued planning happily and it was late when they left the top deck. The moon was shining from a clear sky and it seemed to Jill that its golden path across the water was a symbol of the way ahead for herself and David.

Doctor Nurse Romances

Doctor Nurse Romances

Romance in the wide world of medicine

Amongst the intense emotional pressures of modern medical life, doctors and nurses often find romance. Read about their lives and loves in the other two Doctor Nurse titles available this month.

CAPTIVE HEART
by Hazel Fisher

Sister Catherine Grainger knows that the Bellington District General Hospital is lucky to have the services of their new consultant, Johnnie Kirkland. She also knows the hospital is not big enough for both of them and she will have to go!

A PROFESSIONAL SECRET
by Kate Norway

It is not always easy for doctors and nurses to keep their private lives in separate compartments. Nurse Mary Lee and Dr Euan Carlaw find that trying to do just that lands them in a terrible muddle – especially when they are confronted with a *most* unexpected complication.

Mills & Boon
the rose of romance

 **ROMANCE**

How to join in a whole new world of romance

It's very easy to subscribe to the Mills & Boon Reader Service. As a regular reader, you can enjoy a whole range of special benefits. Bargain offers. Big cash savings. Your own free Reader Service newsletter, packed with knitting patterns, recipes, competitions, and exclusive book offers.

We send you the very latest titles each month, postage and packing free – no hidden extra charges. There's absolutely no commitment – you receive books for only as long as you want.

We'll send you details. Simply send the coupon – or drop us a line for details about the Mills & Boon Reader Service Subscription Scheme.
Post to: Mills & Boon Reader Service, P.O. Box 236, Thornton Road, Croydon, Surrey CR9 3RU, England.
*Please note: READERS IN SOUTH AFRICA please write to: Mills & Boon Reader Service of Southern Africa, Private Bag X3010, Randburg 2125, S. Africa.

Please send me details of the Mills & Boon Subscription Scheme.

NAME (Mrs/Miss) _____ EP3

ADDRESS _____

_____

COUNTY/COUNTRY _____ POST/ZIP CODE _____
BLOCK LETTERS, PLEASE

Mills & Boon
the rose of romance